Slick

E. DAVIES

Publisher's Note: This is a work of fiction. Names, characters, places, and incidents are a product of the author's imagination. Locales and public names are sometimes used for atmospheric purposes. Any resemblance to actual people, living or dead, or to businesses, companies, events, institutions, or locales is completely coincidental.

Slick / E. Davies. – 1st ed.
ISBN: 978-1-912245-14-7

"THEY THINK WE'RE A MISTAKE."

"I don't care." Roman was a mistake Oscar had been waiting months to make. With Roman's hand running up his thigh, he wasn't turning back now.

Oscar rolled his head back against the hotel room wall and wondered if there was enough sound-proofing. He also found that he didn't care.

Roman's hotel room in Knoxville was near the gay bars, but they hadn't even made a pretense of going to a bar first. The moment he'd walked into the room, their hands had been all over each other. They hadn't even made it to the bed.

Normally, Oscar might be at Falcon's studio apartment. He was going to be back here for a month, so he might still wind up crashing on his easygoing best friend's couch for a while.

But Falcon had a new boyfriend to keep him busy tonight, which was another reminder of what a bad idea this was—Roman was his best friend's boyfriend's near-brother, whatever the hell that was called. And both of them had tried to get between Roman and Oscar… until now.

Roman's wandering hand reached Oscar's dick, the heel pressing into the hard length and expertly running along the shaft to the tip, squeezing through Oscar's skinny jeans. Oscar slid down the wall a few inches, his knees weakening.

"Fuck!"

"I'd love to," Roman whispered, those blue eyes fixing on his like Roman wanted to eat him up.

And Oscar wanted him to. He'd been texting Roman from New Zealand, then Southeast Asia, then Japan. Once or twice, their paths had nearly crossed—as an airline pilot, Roman bounced around the world the way some people commuted across town.

It had never quite worked out until they were here, back in their hometown, with everyone they knew busy. Nobody had to know the filthy things Oscar wanted to do with Roman. All night long.

"Naked. Now."

Oscar stripped his t-shirt in one fluid movement, rising onto his toes automatically.

Roman smiled at the move, his gaze flickering down Oscar's body from head to toe. "How flexible are you?"

Oscar snorted with amusement. It was always a guy's first question when he found out Oscar was a dancer. "Why don't you find out?"

Roman growled and leaned in to lick slowly from Oscar's collarbone to his ear. "I plan to."

"Aren't you getting naked, too?" Oscar asked, nodding at Roman. He was still in a collared shirt and tie, arousal pressing at his trousers. Keeping his eyes off that was a difficult feat, but Roman's eyes were too captivating to look away from for long.

"Do you want me to?"

That was a good point. He had that classic sex appeal of a man in a suit that was perfectly tailored to fit his broad shoulders and muscled barrel chest.

"You'll roast in that jacket. The rest can stay," Oscar decided.

Roman's lips quirked into a grin. "I thought you'd say that. Judging by your reaction to my texts, anyway."

Their texts back and forth had included photos. Never any dirty ones, but definitely suggestive enough for jerk-off material. Oscar's were in leotards and tights, after all, which showcased all of his assets. Roman's had been largely of suits, and Oscar was fairly sure he hadn't worn underwear in any of them.

Oscar dropped his pants and underwear, leaving his socks on. His feet didn't hurt today, but nobody wanted toughened toes dragging against their leg in bed. His cock stood straight up already as he shifted from foot to foot, wriggling against the wall. "Gonna show me what you've got?"

The pop of the button and the purr of Roman's zipper sliding down sent shivers of anticipation through Oscar. When Roman finally eased it out, it didn't disappoint. The thick, veined length in Roman's hand would fill him to his limit, but Oscar was well used to stretching of all kinds.

Warmth tingled through Oscar's body, down to the tips of his toes. He wanted to jump on right now.

"You got lube?"

"Lucky for you..." Roman made a show of reaching into

the interior pocket of his jacket, pulling out condom and a flat tube of KY before tossing the jacket aside.

Oscar snorted with laughter. "Showoff. Do you keep that on you 24/7?"

"You never know when an opportunity will present itself. And speaking of presenting itself..." Roman held out the lube.

Oscar turned to face the wall and spread his legs while Roman's hands wandered up the backs of his thighs to squeeze his hard-won asset. "So firm," Roman breathed out. "I loved your photos."

"I know you did," Oscar grinned, batting Roman's hand aside so he could press slick fingers into himself. He took his own turn making a show of fucking himself slowly on his fingers, rippling his back smoothly with each push back into them. He wanted to see how long it would take to drive Roman nuts.

Not long. Roman growled after a minute and pressed his cock to Oscar's entrance, so Oscar let his fingers slide out and guided the tip against, then into, him. "Mmm," Oscar breathed out, taking an inch at a time of that thick shaft.

"Oh! Jesus. You're fuckin' good," Roman hissed. Roman brushed his hand aside and took over, filling Oscar with the burning heat he so loved. It was too slow, though, too much of a tease, to have him gently working his way inside.

Oscar flattened his hands against the wall and backed into Roman. "Fuck me."

"Are you ready?"

Roman really didn't know him. Dancers had stupidly high pain tolerance, and he was spreadeagled under some guy more often than Roman probably guessed. Hell, Oscar *could* fuck without lube, but not as hard and fast as he wanted Roman to go tonight. He was glad Roman thought ahead. "More than. Hurry the fuck up."

Picking up on the cue, Roman ran his hand up Oscar's back and grabbed his hair, pulling his head back as he slammed his hips forward.

Thickness and fullness coursed through Oscar, his skin burning. He moaned loudly with each quick, deep thrust, melting under Roman's attention. The nails digging into his hip burned so nicely, to say nothing of the manhood stretching him open and rubbing his prostate—thanks to the careful hip angle he maintained.

Each thrust sent sparks of need through him, and Oscar had to shift his focus to holding out against the orgasm that was crashing toward him far too fast.

"Yes, yes, *yes*!" he hissed to encourage Roman. The firm slap against his ass made his knees buckle before he caught himself and arched again, pushing back into Roman.

They were sweaty and hot now, and as Roman crushed Oscar to the wall with his chest, Oscar turned his head sideways so his cheek pressed the cold wall. Roman's beautiful eyes were mostly closed, but his lips were parted, and he looked fucking *gorgeous*.

Next round, Oscar wanted to be facing him.

As if sensing his thoughts, Roman's eyes flickered open and met his, and his lips brushed Oscar's in a long, dirty kiss. Then, he pulled back and whispered, "I'm gonna fuck you all night long."

"You'd better," Oscar moaned, squeezing around Roman as arousal flushed through him again, making his skin prickle with urgency. "Oh, fuck. Yes!"

Then Roman's hand closed around his throbbing cock and he just about lost his mind. All he cared about was the way his head spun and his body burned with every thrust, and the way their hot skin rubbed smoothly with the sweat between their bodies. The weight of Roman pushing him into the wall, pinning him there with his cock and every damn toned inch of his body.

A moan slipped from Oscar's throat, and when he tossed his head back, Roman's lips were there, sucking on his neck and ear, overwhelming every fucking nerve in his body.

If this was a mistake, Oscar didn't care even a bit. He came harder than he could remember doing in ages, thrusting into Roman's tight grip and backing into his swelling cock.

Roman grunted and sucked Oscar's neck before he came. His voice broke mid-cry and he breathed Oscar's name so quietly Oscar could almost swear he imagined it as his cock relentlessly pounded into Oscar's body with erratic, needy thrusts.

When Roman softened and pulled out, he shrugged off the rest of his clothes in quick movements and nodded to the bed.

"All night?" Oscar smirked and raised his brows to make sure Roman had really meant it.

Apparently it hadn't been the heat of the moment. As Roman tossed the condom in the trash, he cast Oscar a sultry grin that made heat coil within his belly, even though his passion was splattered across the wall and his libido hadn't quite caught up to another round. "I like to make mistakes several times, just to make sure."

Oscar flopped on the bed and idly stroked his sensitive cock, then pulled Roman against him. "May as well make the most of it."

He suspected Roman was just the same as him—they

didn't form bonds. And it was clear Falcon and Blane disapproved of the possibility of them breaking each other's heart. No doubt the rest of Roman's friendship circle that Falcon had been welcomed into felt the same.

Plus, their lifestyles. Who could make that work? Not them, that was for sure.

Once they'd hooked up tonight, it was probably it. So yeah, Oscar was going to take advantage of every damn second.

He closed his eyes and shivered as Roman's hands wandered down his sides, grazing his ribs and exploring the firmness of his ass again. "Keep that up and I'll be ready to go again."

Roman responded with a single word, but the way he growled it into Oscar's ear made his nerves light up with desire all over again.

"Good."

CHAPTER

One

ROMAN

"I'M JEALOUS. YOU CAN GET SOME GUY TO SUCK YOU OFF FOR nothing at some sleazy bar, can't you? I gotta pretend I *like* some chick for more than her tits."

Roman had to fight to keep his expression neutral. It was just banter, but the attitude wound him up. Not only was Cory a dick about women in general, but his comments had been turning increasingly homophobic since he'd made first officer. Being gay wasn't all about easy fucking for everyone —Roman just happened to like no-strings-attached hookups, and that was that. If he could find a guy to say, "I do," he'd always known that would change.

Meanwhile Cory acted like he didn't want any of it. He had two girlfriends and didn't love either of them. Hell, he didn't even seem to *like* them.

Roman kept his comment to, "The grass is always greener."

Cory took it the wrong way, of course. "You ever try this side of the fence? Just a munch?" he grinned.

Roman fought back the urge to punch him. It wouldn't

look good on his flight record. "I dated a girl in high school. A couple of my friends are bi, I wanted to make sure I wasn't. I already knew, but just for science. Why, have you tried *this* side? Something you wanna tell me?"

The jab worked. Cory looked suddenly defensive and scowled at him. "I'm not gay, man. You know that."

There was a knock on the door, and one of the flight attendants poked her head in. "Everything all right?"

Pre-flight checks. That would take his mind off wanting to verbally eviscerate the man sitting next to him. "Fine, thanks. Sorry. Where were we?" Roman said pointedly, and his copilot took the hint.

It was all routine to both of them by now, but airlines didn't count on that. Pilots had checklists for a reason. One slip of the mind, the other guy not catching it, and tragedy could occur otherwise.

Checks and cross-checks complete, it was time to do his job. For a few minutes, even Cory's unprofessionalism gave way to the responsibility placed in their hands.

Several thousand flight hours later, the same adrenaline coursed through him every time, only to be held in check by his training. It was time for takeoff.

Cruising altitude, post-takeoff checks complete, Cory seemed to have forgotten his earlier banter. At least Roman had been able to get a good morning's sleep-in to deal with him after... well.

After last night.

"What are your plans in Hong Kong?"

It was due to be a long, boring flight over the Pacific

today, and they were sharing the cockpit on the way back, so Roman figured he might as well try to get along with the guy. They had several hours together before the next shift of pilots came on-duty, after all. Neither of them would be landing—one of the other pilots had to, for status reasons.

"Nothing planned, really," he said, trying to drag his mind away from the night with Oscar. "Why, you have anything?" As far as he knew, Cory didn't have a girl in this port of call yet.

"We'll probably be too tired to get up to anything fun," Cory groused. "And we can't on the last night, either. That's really only one good night there, you know? Long-haul sucks."

"I hate rules as much as the next guy, but hey," Roman shrugged. "They *are* rules." It was a less-than-subtle hint that he *would* report Cory for getting up to any bullshit. "There's always tonic water."

"Gross. I should have known you'd like tonic water."

"*Like* is a strong word." Roman half-smiled.

Normally he'd find a group of new friends for the night, get drunk if time allowed, or at least help them to, and find a hot guy to take home for the night.

This time, though, the urge wasn't there. Last night *had* been pretty damn awesome.

"You're looking like the cat who got the cream. Or someone's cream, anyway," Cory snickered.

I'm sure they stop the flight clock if you assault another officer. "Hey, man. If you're jealous, I can show you the best spots when we get there."

Cory laughed. "Gross. I'm not that desperate."

"Mm." Roman checked the flight instruments to give himself a minute to calm down before he saw red.

Not for the first time, he considered talking to someone about it. Telling HR, or one of the senior captains who could have a word in Cory's ear. God, just venting to a friend about it—except he knew better than to think any coworkers were friends.

He'd earned the coveted long-haul route on a combination of talent and willingness to be away from home for long stretches. Among the younger crew, long-haul routes were the most popular; the older guys liked spending nights at home with their families. But, he reminded himself, he was new all over again here... this was hazing. If he went to anyone about it, it would only get worse.

So Roman gritted his teeth and changed the subject to Christmas plans, hoping the next couple hours until the next shift went quickly.

Or he was gonna get in real trouble.

CHAPTER

Two

OSCAR

AUTOPILOT WAS THE FIRST, AND MOST JUNIOR, MISTAKE NEW dancers made during company classes. Following moves without thinking about them was a recipe for disaster. That way, you couldn't adjust as needed for healing injuries or weaknesses. A small misstep could be the end of a promising career.

It took all Oscar's concentration to keep to the music today. Now that his company was back in Knoxville, they were working through routines to stay in shape, but more importantly, it was a competition. Raj, the creative director, was going to judge who to cast in the principal role of the next show.

The decision was due any day now. Oscar had gotten good reviews worldwide. He'd moved past another face in the ensemble to distinguish himself, and he worked damn hard to keep that up.

He never missed a class, and in three seasons, had never missed a show. He'd danced through injuries, which won him even more acclaim from his directors, and the envy of some fellow dancers.

Oscar's eyes slid sideways to Jef. This dance routine suited him much better. Oscar had trained primarily in ballet and then contemporary dance, but he struggled to keep up with this beat. It fit Jef's tribal fusion and musical theater background far better.

Jef's body moved fluidly, his hip snapping at just the right moment, emphasizing the curve next to it in his leotard.

Oscar gritted his teeth, reminding himself yet again to count the beats and not think about anyone else. Another elementary rule.

He fixed his eyes on himself in the mirror, trying to keep the beat moving through his body even in the split-seconds between movements, but he looked forced to his own eye. He relaxed, but now he just looked slightly too slow to keep up with the company.

"Five, six, seven, eight, and—good."

Raj was not going to let him get away with this. As he walked between dancers, Raj tapped shoulders one at a time.

"You won't get anywhere on floppy feet. Keep your back straighter. Turn the right way, for God's sake." Raj had reached him, and Oscar winced, but all Raj said was, "Talk to me after class."

Oscar's head spun. That couldn't be a good sign. *Dance*, he told himself as he finished the song like he hadn't heard anything. *Just fucking dance.*

The music ended, they cooled off, and Raj was at the front of the class. "How about something classic?" They all recognized Swan Lake.

With this one, Oscar *could* let his conscious mind go and

lose himself in the rhythm. A hundred dance classes came back to him—being eleven, his dad dropping him off after his custody weekends, using the music to forget the looks his mom and dad had shot each other when he picked him up. Eight, when he'd realized dance spoke to him in a way no other creative art did. Seventeen, auditioning for school…

A smile slipped across Oscar's face as he stepped, turned, leapt. Plies were as natural as breathing to him. It took him half the routine before he even remembered to look at Jef. Just as he had a few minutes ago, Jef was struggling with this one.

Raj was walking up and down between rows of dancers, reminding those few who needed it of the steps.

Oscar didn't need the reminder—or any corrections. Raj walked silently past him and Oscar let the pride flow through him for a few moments. In a company class, silence was a compliment.

The music hit a crescendo, and he pirouetted, leapt, stepped, leapt again. The easiest way to express emotion was through his body. He'd never known a better way. The voice failed, but the body told the truth.

When the music ended, it left him strangely wistful. He glanced sideways at Jef again, who was already walking away to stretch and drink water. They joked around as they cooled off, keeping one ear on Raj for the debrief.

That passed quickly, too. Oscar hardly paid attention, he was so worried about what might be coming next.

As everyone else left, Jef and he were the only two remaining.

Oh, shit. They don't have a problem with us, do they?

Plenty of dancers hooked up. Sometimes long-term. Hell,

some got married. He and Jef hadn't let their sexual tension or the occasional relief thereof interfere with the shows or even rehearsal. Besides, it made a good release valve for the competitive pressure that easily built between them. If it was shallow, at least the attraction was mutual.

"I won't beat around the bush. We're looking at either of you for the principal role. It isn't strictly in either of your wheelhouses, but we're confident either of you could learn it. The choreography will challenge either of you."

Oscar felt the blood pounding in his ears. Whatever they required, he'd learn it. Hell, he'd put in the extra hours to get better as fast as they needed him to—faster.

"But I'm not bringing you together to make this a petty one-upmanship competition," Raj added instantly, with a warning look. "Keep it off stage."

"Oh—"

"No—"

He and Jef rushed to assure Raj at the same moment that there was no problem.

None at all.

"Right," Raj said after a moment, looking between them. "Anyway, that's all I wanted to say. Good work today, guys. Go get changed."

They were nowhere near alone in the changing room, and by mutual if silent agreement, neither of them wanted to bring it up within earshot of anyone else.

Both men dragged their heels through stripping, showering, drying off, and dressing again. It gave Oscar a chance to sort out his thoughts about the whole thing, and Jef was probably in the same place.

Leading the production. Can you even imagine? It made a chill run down Oscar's spine. He'd fought for this chance for so long, and now that it was here, he was pitted against his... well, sometimes-lover, sometimes-rival. There was no word that encapsulated their relationship.

"That's that, then," Jef said, drawing Oscar's attention as he zipped his knapsack shut.

"Huh?" Jef jerked his chin around the empty changing room, and Oscar caught on and nodded. "Yeah." He shouldered his bag and reached a hand out to shake. "Good luck, man. If they choose you... you'll be great."

"I was just thinking the same." Jef crookedly smiled.

Oscar could see in Jef what he didn't in himself, and for perhaps the first time, he realized that Jef might feel the same way about him. He stared for a moment too long at Jef's lips, waiting for him to say anything else.

"Good luck to you, too." Jef pulled back and stepped around him, giving him a wide berth for the first time... ever, maybe.

Oscar felt weirdly empty. He'd half-expected a hug, and half of that part of him had expected a knife in the back after the hug. Or a knife in the back and then a hug. Or just one or the other, for now. Like a Punnett square of dance rivalry.

With his mind caught up in his metaphor, before he could say anything else, Jef was gone.

Oscar walked slowly toward the entrance of the studio, his mind on his practice routine. He had to step it up if he was going to get picked—study what Jef did and copy it? If they were looking for a blend of their strengths, he had to step outside his comfort zone and show them he could do it.

And then his foot slipped sideways on the marble step down to the sidewalk, the ground rushing up to meet him as something popped in his knee.

Motherfucker!

His knee flared with pain as it buckled, but his expression showed nothing. Years of training to dance through pain kept his last step to the sidewalk smooth even though his other knee wouldn't bend without an agonizing fire throughout the joint, and his fingers curled so tightly around the railing that his knuckles turned white.

"Oscar. Shit. Are you okay?"

Raj's hand was on his shoulder, guiding him to sit on the step, supporting his bad leg.

Oscar's world collapsed around him.

He saw it all. I can't hide it now. Fuck. Can I play it off?

As his knee straightened, Oscar hissed in pain, then gritted his teeth as red-hot frustration surged through him at his reaction. "I'm fine."

"No, you're not." Raj spoke with the patient experience of a man who'd watched his dancers push through all manner of injuries—someone who would look past the careful mask of art to the subtle signs. Oscar's fingertips dug into the step on either side of him, and Raj couldn't miss the pale sheen to his skin and his quick breathing.

Not like this.

Oscar bent over his knee, supporting it with both hands as he tried to straighten it.

"Whoa. Don't push it." Raj crouched next to him, fingers pressing into the joint as he looked up at Oscar.

When his fingers pressed around the kneecap, they caused another flare of pain so intense it overshadowed the pride burning its way out from his heart.

"Fuck!"

Raj hissed and patted his shin gently. "It's your kneecap, honey."

"I fucking know it's my fucking kneecap. I'm fucking *fine*."

The door banged shut behind him, and Oscar didn't even turn to look. He could feel who it was, and he wanted the world to rewind thirty seconds. *Why now?*

Jef's steps clattered down the stairs and he paused, half-crouching next to him. "What happened?"

Raj waved a hand to dismiss him. "We've got it under control." Oscar straightened up, wiggling his toes and shifting his weight as if it were a minor strain, and Raj eyed him. "I'm not fooled, Oscar."

Jef lingered near the bottom of the stairs. "Need a hand?"

"We're fine, thanks," Raj repeated, turning to look at him. "See you tomorrow." It was closer to *fuck off* than Oscar had expected, and he appreciated the protection, but there was no hiding Jef's reaction.

Jef gave him an ambiguous smile. "See you around." He walked off, a spring in his step.

Twist the knife, why don't you, little fucker. Oscar glared after him.

Raj put an arm around him. "Up you get. We need to get you x-rayed. But you know what this means."

"Six weeks recovery? Eight?" Oscar was miserable.

"Yep."

Oscar's voice shook as he rose to his feet, and he was willing to pretend it was the physical pain causing that. "I'm out, aren't I?"

"Yeah, hon." Raj helped him to the side street where his car was parked. "You're financially okay to do that, right?"

Oscar nodded. Thankfully, he'd always kept his head on straight and saved most of what he made in case of exactly this. Most dancers were injured sooner or later, and without incoming money from performances, they could find themselves screwed very fast.

Raj sensed his distress. After Oscar was settled in the passenger seat, he climbed into the driver's side. "You have a long and promising career. Don't fuck it up for one tour."

Oscar turned his head to look out the window, not trusting his voice enough to answer.

"Of course he's not home."

Oscar bumped his head against the door. The long walk up to the studio loft—more pulling himself upstairs, really—had been frustrating on his own.

But it wasn't the worst injury he'd ever had, and without Raj there, he didn't have to smile through the pain and look elegant. Oscar had insisted he was fine to get inside to his friend's place, conveniently not mentioning that his friend lived on the top floor.

Still, he caught himself wishing Falcon were here just to bring him a cup of coffee or a beer while he was laid up.

It was lonely here, even in the pretty, airy, well-lit studio apartment surrounded by Falcon's very presence in the form of all the artwork, that finished and that still drying. But his and Blane's house move was pending, and this wouldn't last much longer.

He didn't blame Falcon for wanting to spend all the time he could with his boyfriend. New love was a powerful force.

Almost enough to make him jealous. What he and Jef had wasn't love—not even close. It was laughably stereotypical: rivals toeing the line between enmity and lust.

It didn't make it less real, though, and it didn't make him

less likely to say yes the next time they shared a hotel room on tour.

That smile, though? He wanted to punch Jef for it. So far below the belt that there was no even joking about it.

"Fuck you, and fuck your stupid leading-man face."

CHAPTER
Three
ROMAN

Roman wasn't *planning* to hook up tonight. He'd just gotten back to town yesterday. With several nights in a row here, he was staying at home rather than getting a hotel to bring someone back to.

He rarely brought anyone back to his place. It was out in the suburbs—way easier to grab a hotel for a wild night. He was just looking in on the bar to see who was around.

It shouldn't have been such a surprise to see Oscar at the gay bar. Knoxville wasn't exactly overflowing with said gay bars or gays in said bars, so the odds were good.

It *was* a surprise to see him downing a shot while holding another in reserve in the other hand. Before Roman even made it over to the bar, both shot glasses sat empty on the counter, and Oscar's eyes were closed as he rode the high.

Roman leaned in to whisper in his ear, "Boo."

Oscar gasped and slipped off his stool. "Motherfucker!"

It was a good thing Roman caught him, hands on his waist and shoulder to pull him upright again until he had his balance. "Getting a dancer off-balance has to be a rare feat."

Oscar swayed slightly under his touch, so he kept his hands there. "You all right?"

"Fuckin' fine."

Roman snorted and slid his hands off that gorgeous, slender body with great reluctance, taking the stool next to him. "That sounds like a lie."

"Well done."

Oof. He had some prickle to him today. Roman tilted his head and looked at him, then flagged down the bartender. "Two Cokes, please."

"Maybe I don't want a Coke." It sounded sullen, not offended, though.

"You had a Coke the first time we met."

Oscar rolled his eyes but accepted the drink. Finally, he turned to actually look at Roman, his gaze thoughtful.

He looked like shit, but Roman was pretty sure he'd earn a slap for saying so. Instead, he studied Oscar for a moment before his eyes dropped to the bulge around his knee. Bandages? "What happened?"

"Just a minor dislocation." Oscar's tone was deeply bitter, though.

Roman didn't really know how to proceed. "Oh. Shit. Sorry."

"Enough whiskey and I'll pretend I'm over it. Oh, yeah. And then I have to go home."

"Where's home?" Roman asked. Surely he hadn't been away for long enough for Oscar to get an apartment here. For that matter, what *did* he do when he was back in town?

"Falcon's place. The studio loft." Oscar sounded miserable as he looked down at his knee.

It clicked: his best friend's boyfriend's place was at the top of a rickety old building. No way did it have an elevator.

Sharing that studio had to be uncomfortable in good health, let alone with an injury.

"Come home with me." Roman didn't even know where it came from—it just slipped out, like many of his words.

He didn't mean it sexually, though Oscar had teased Roman throughout his time in Hong Kong with dirty photos, apparently not contented with one hookup as the culmination of all that sexual tension.

Oscar's head snapped up and he stared at him. "What? I can't…"

"Why not? I don't mind. I've got a spare room. We can keep it all nice and clean and tame for our friends," Roman smirked at him.

Oscar's eyelids were heavy—what hour was it by now, anyway? And how long had he been in here mainlining alcohol?

"In any case, you gotta get out of here, and I'm not carrying your ass up the stairs."

That got a reaction. Oscar drew himself up to his full height on the stool and backward, looking down his nose at Roman—as much as he could, since Roman was several inches taller. "I never asked you to carry me."

"Well, I'm not letting you drag your own ass up there, either. How many flights of stairs is it?"

"I've had worse."

"Not the point." Roman got to his feet and offered Oscar his arm.

Oscar sneered at it and stood up. He immediately braced himself on the stool and the bar, then carefully let go.

"Pride," Roman said softly. "It won't get you anywhere."

Oscar shifted his weight onto both feet, his face suspiciously blank. "Except into cute guys' pants, all over the world. Right? It worked on me."

"No, that's ego and a slick attitude," Roman smirked. "In between committing too fast and scaring every goddamn boyfriend off." He leaned in, wrapping an arm around Oscar's shoulders to support him. "And *that's* jealousy." Distracting Oscar from the pain was all he could do. *The idiot better not be on painkillers* and *drinking.*

His concern for Oscar was… brotherly. That was what he told himself, anyway.

"No," Oscar mumbled, but his cheeks flushed. He finally leaned on Roman, and they headed for the door. His weight was slight, but the warm, firm presence by his side made Roman's chest warm in turn. "Where do you live?"

"Not really the heart of the city." It was Roman's turn to be briefly embarrassed. His house was nothing to be ashamed of, but it was so… well, cozy. Homely. Not the bachelor pad most people would have associated his name with.

"Suburbia? I wouldn't have thought it."

"Houses were cheap, and I wasn't paying downtown rent for a place I'm not in half the time."

Oscar hummed. "Makes sense. Like me, crashing with Falcon for a couple months out of the year. Some people split AirBNBs or stay with their parents or whatever."

"Your company tours a lot, then," Roman observed as they stepped into the chilly evening together. "Don't most dancers do a couple tours a year or something? If that?"

"It depends on the company, yeah." Oscar's speech was clear, at least, and he wasn't swaying on his feet. He wasn't quite the mess he'd seemed inside—at least, not now that he was talking about his company. It occurred to Roman then that dwelling on it was a bad idea.

"Oh, cool. So, where's Falcon?" Roman asked.

"Probably Pier 1. Or Bed, Bath, Behind, whatever they call it." Oscar rolled his eyes.

Roman laughed. "They are kind of grossly sweet together, aren't they?"

Oscar was quiet for a moment as Roman led him around the corner to the side street where he'd parked. When Roman looked over at him again, he was surprised to see wet streaks on his cheeks.

"What's wrong?" Roman asked, his brows knitting.

Oscar swiped at his cheeks and coughed. "Doesn't matter."

"It does. Don't make me keep asking. I'm not very patient," Roman advised him. "Or, worse yet, start guessing."

Oscar shook his head, his gaze down on his bulging knee again. Roman's guess was that it was a splint under his jeans. "I'm screwed. I'm so fucking screwed. I can't practice, I can't dance, I can't do jack shit for two months. I'm used to working out every day! I'll be fat and ugly and unemployed and I won't even be able to do a split. Who the fuck wants to date that?"

Roman stopped dead, then stifled his laugh for a second. It didn't work, though, and his laugh rolled through him.

Oscar glared at him. "What?"

"You? Ugly? Never."

Oscar's cheeks flushed, but he still looked annoyed as he stared around at the street signs instead.

"Fat? Doesn't mean anything. A little extra padding makes the ride better," Roman winked, pulling Oscar into his side and squeezing his ass.

"Should've known you'd be molesting me," Oscar muttered, but he was starting to smile. "Fuck you, I'm trying to be… pissed off at the world."

Roman hummed and rested his chin on Oscar's head. The moment Oscar leaned into him, he drew him into both arms and pulled him into his chest, an instinctive reaction so deep-rooted he didn't even think twice before he did it. He just wanted Oscar to feel better.

"You've spent hours doing that already, didn't you?" Roman asked. "I'm not gonna let you mope. And seriously, dude. *Nobody will want me if I can't do a split?*" Roman started laughing again.

Faintly at first, as if reluctant, Oscar chuckled, then joined in. "Fuck off. I know my assets."

"You sure do," Roman said. Before he could get a good grope in, the sound of passersby at the end of the alley made Oscar step back from him. Roman playfully pouted, then told him, "Come on. My car's here. I'll let you have one more diva moment, but only after I'm home with a beer in my hand."

Oscar dramatically sighed and wiped his cheeks again, but he was smiling as Roman helped him into the passenger seat. "Asshole."

"You know it." Roman grinned at him and shut the door.

"Did you want a glass of water before I let you have your second dramatic moment?"

Oscar glared at Roman, but he couldn't keep it up for longer than a few seconds before he cracked and laughed. "It's a good thing I like the bad boys."

"Do you?" Roman smiled, kicking his shoes off and leaned on the doorway, hooking his thumbs into the belt loops of his jeans. "Maybe I need to be more of a jerk, then." He lowered his voice to a growl. "You want water or a good fuck?"

Oscar smirked. He could tell Roman was playing the clown to amuse him, but there was no way he'd pass the chance up. After all, their sex last time had been fucking *hot*. "Yes, sir, if you please."

They made eye contact for a few moments longer, Roman's eyes widening and then slowly narrowing as he clearly thought over the idea.

Gotcha. Oscar hid his smile as Roman swallowed hard and turned away. "Kitchen's this way."

"Mmm." Oscar followed close on his heels. With the knee brace and years of developing a high pain tolerance, he only had a slight limp.

Nevertheless, Roman pulled out a chair at the kitchen island for him and ushered him into it with more hands than, strictly speaking, *needed* to be on his body.

Oscar swallowed his own reaction, trying to will away the prickling heat in his body. They had at least all night—weeks, maybe, if Roman was serious about letting him stay here.

That reminded him to look around at the kitchen, checking out how it was decorated. You could tell a lot about a man from his home, Oscar had always thought.

Very cozy, down to the painting of a bowl of fruit hanging near the stove. He hid a smile. "This isn't what I expected. It's a lot less..."

"Bachelor pad?" Roman finished with a sigh. "I know. This is why I don't bring guys back here."

"You have an image to maintain?" Oscar took the glass of water, their hands brushing as Roman leaned against the island next to him. He sipped slowly.

Roman looked embarrassed for a moment. "I... uh. I guess? Anyway, there are some things that need fixing." He waved a hand around. "I'm tearing out the kitchen cupboards sometime, that kind of stuff. It'll be sleeker in a few years."

"All that and a handyman, too," Oscar teased.

Roman's cheeks flushed and he stared at his glass. "On occasion."

Oscar couldn't drag his eyes off Roman's face. For such a confident man—brash, even, from their first meeting—he had this dimension to him that he couldn't figure out yet. "You really don't mind me staying here?"

That got his attention. "Oh, of course not." Roman looked at him. "Seriously, the guest room never gets used. And it's renovated. I shouldn't have done it first. Nobody comes to visit anyway, aside from Nico, and now he stays with Deen. Should've done the damn kitchen instead," he grumbled, then chuckled. "But I guess it came in handy at last."

"I guess so." Oscar turned to face him, setting aside the water glass. "Listen, I really appreciate it. Even if I'm Falcon's best friend and whatever… you don't have to."

"Stop trying to talk me out of it." Roman ran his hand up Oscar's arm from his elbow to his shoulder in a gentle, affectionate touch. "You obviously can't stay on the top floor of a building with your knee in that shape. Does he know, anyway?"

"Not yet. He vanishes for days at time these days. No wonder they're moving in together." Oscar didn't mention that he hadn't texted Falcon because he wasn't sure how to break the news: *I dislocated my kneecap walking down some stairs and fucked over my whole life.* No, he had to wait to talk to him in person.

Roman smirked. "Yeah. No point paying rent if they're nesting at Blane's house all the time."

Oscar chuckled, noticing that Roman still hadn't moved his hand from his shoulder. "Imagine what they'll think: us, living together. Only question is, which of us breaks the other's heart? And who kicks whose ass?"

"I think it'll just be an all-out brawl," Roman decided, grinning. "Are the rumors true, then?"

"Are *yours* true?" Oscar countered, sliding his knees along the outsides of Roman's thighs to pull him between his legs. "Flying all over the world, breaking hearts as you go…"

Roman scoffed. "That's a second date question, at least."

"Are we not on our second date?" Oscar smirked. "Second fuck, I was hoping."

He couldn't grip Roman's waist with his knees like he normally might, but he raised his good leg to wrap around his waist, his arms around Roman's shoulders. He balanced his other heel on the rung of the chair.

With the length of his body pressed against Roman's, Roman pushed against him as he'd hoped, his back pressing into the kitchen island as they ground together slowly.

"Some men might call you easy," Roman commented, his eyes sparkling. "I like easy."

Oscar winked. "Takes one to know one. Are you gonna show me my bedroom now? And that good fuck you promised earlier?"

"Come here, trouble," Roman told him. He slid his hands under Oscar's ass and hoisted him up, his grip rock-solid.

Oscar relaxed into him, still half-tense in case of a trip-and-fall or clumsy moment, but instinctively trusting Roman to keep him safe. It was frustrating not to be able to lock his ankles around Roman's waist, but he tried not to dwell on it.

Roman carried him like a feather despite Oscar's deceptively slender body of solid muscle. He couldn't deny that being manhandled like this did things for him. Oscar's cock was already twitching into a hard line against Roman's stomach.

"I thought of you a lot in the cockpit on the way back here," Roman murmured. "They don't call it a cockpit for nothing."

Oscar shivered and pressed his face into Roman's neck, breathing in his cologne. "The photos I sent?"

Clearly, he'd made the right call to stay in touch after their hot hookup. The energy between them was every bit as intense as it had been last time he'd found himself in Roman's arms, not even two weeks ago now. A week? Time had slid by without his even noticing.

"Yeah, those photos, you little minx." Roman shouldered through a doorway and dumped him on the bed. He didn't even give him the chance to look around. He was already hauling Oscar's shirt off, his gaze hungry—no, famished. "You know how hard it is to silently jerk off in the crew bathroom?"

Oscar nearly ripped Roman's shirt off in return, the need to see him shirtless making him almost incoherent. He'd been longing for those huge biceps and firm abs since their first hookup. He restrained himself at the last moment. Roman didn't seem the type to appreciate his expensive dress shirt buttons getting pulled off willy-nilly. "About as hard as jerking off in the group showers at rehearsals."

A few seconds' patience gave him what he was looking for: Roman's bare chest pressed against his, crushing him into the bed. Roman's lips followed immediately. "Not sorry," he mumbled into Oscar's mouth, then sucked his lower lip hard and bit it. "You deserve a good, hard fuck for all that teasing."

Oscar whimpered and bucked against Roman's body, but that just ground their hard lengths together. "I do. And you should be the one to do it."

"That's exactly what I was thinking." Roman was already pulling Oscar's jeans down, going extra-carefully around his knee and when working them over his feet, then straddling his hips again.

"Thanks," Oscar murmured, watching him unbutton and unzip his own trousers.

"Huh?" Roman paused and looked at him, his brow furrowed with confusion.

"For not just bashing my knee around."

"I don't know what kind of guys you've been fucking, but I'll knock their heads together if they hurt you."

Oscar laughed under his breath. "Not deliberately. They just don't seem to..." *Care, I almost said. Too honest? Probably.* "Think," he finished instead.

"Most guys don't think with the right brain," Roman agreed with an upward quirk of his lip. "It's a shame they're so hot I can't keep my hands off." He ran his hands up Oscar's bare stomach and chest for emphasis. "And I keep trying to marry them, for some goddamn reason. Probably the unlimited sex. Haven't found one to say yes yet, don't worry."

Oscar laughed again, his heart light. Despite everything—despite his shitty afternoon and worse evening, until Roman walked through the door and made everything better—he could almost forget about it now. With Roman's hands on him, his calm and confident demeanor was like permission to relax.

And relax Oscar did, even though he was tense with arousal. He grinned as he watched Roman fight his trousers off like an unwanted hug in a bar. "You're adorable."

Roman looked more surprised at this than he had a moment ago. "I don't usually... I mean, people don't usually..." he trailed off.

Oscar smiled. "Tell you that? Well, it's true." He could see how Roman was in danger of being the hot playboy hunk, but there was this new and fascinating side to him, too—easily frustrated in tiny matters, but cool-headed in large ones, and shy about showing off his home. Something about him was intriguing in a way Oscar hadn't felt before.

Roman didn't say anything, but his cheeks were red. He pinched Oscar's nipple and rolled it between his fingers.

"Oof!" Oscar exclaimed, his body jerking, but not unpleasantly so. In fact, a tingle of arousal shot straight to his cock. "Fine. I won't tell you you're adorable… you hot, kinky bastard."

Roman grinned. "Better," he said with a laugh. He leaned down to kiss the sensitive nub, then the other one. That also lined their cocks up for the perfect grinding motion.

They both felt it at once and pushed against each other, the tip of Roman's cock already slick against Oscar's shaft.

"There! Yes," Oscar gasped when the veiny shaft rubbed against the head of his own just right, sending a thrill of pleasure through him.

Roman rubbed his body against Oscar's, harder this time. Their cocks were trapped between their stomachs now, rubbing back and forth just slow enough not to sting as slickness covered them both.

"You like that?" Roman growled. "I can feel you getting even harder." He licked his palm and knelt up enough to fit his hand between them, then stroked their cocks to make it easier.

Oscar whimpered and nodded when Roman pushed his hips forward again, almost experimentally, and easily slid along Oscar's cock. That felt even better, and his nails dug into the back of Roman's hips, then into his ass as he kneaded it. "You can fuck me anytime, gorgeous."

"Yeah," Roman grunted his pleasure. "I love fucking you, too. You squirm so much."

Oscar hadn't even realized he was pushing up against Roman and wriggling, making Roman's job harder. He blushed and tried to settle down, but the next thrust sent sparks dancing along his skin, all the way to his fingers and toes. He wriggled again with pleasure. "Oh, I could come just like this."

"Really?" Roman's eyes lit up with a devilish gleam.

Oscar caught his breath and moaned as Roman thrust harder, faster, his hands resting on Oscar's shoulder and hip to hold him still against the bed. "Oh, yeah. Oh, *fuck*." He suddenly couldn't breathe. His toes curled into the bed with every thrust.

It felt like Roman stretched it out forever specifically to tease him—dragged his body against Oscar's, slow and steady and relentless, however much Oscar begged and squirmed—before he pushed harder and faster.

"Oscar," Roman growled, between his gasps for breath. "Wanna feel you come, baby. I'm gonna make a hell of a mess."

"Been holding out for me?" Oscar teased, and he was suddenly even more breathless as Roman hesitated to answer. He *really* hadn't expected this.

Roman finally half-shrugged and kissed him until he was out of breath and moaning into Roman's mouth, desperately seeking another caress of Roman's tongue against his lips.

His body tightened and pushed against Roman's, his body spilling its passion across them both. Roman kissed him *hard*, swallowing his moans. Then, Roman thrust a few more times, flexing that incredible ass effortlessly until his warmth shot across them both—plentifully, like he'd warned him.

Oscar's brain switched back on as he realized they were wet and sweaty, Roman collapsed where he was and pressing him into the bed. He looped his arms around Roman's waist and kissed his neck, his mind suddenly back to those words a minute ago.

"Yeah," Roman muttered.

"Huh?"

"Yeah, I was holding out, I guess. I just didn't feel like it in Hong Kong." Roman sounded gruff, like he wouldn't have minded not admitting it, which made Oscar wonder why he *was* saying it.

Instead, Oscar swallowed his curiosity and kissed Roman a few more times. "Was it worth the wait? You didn't even get inside me."

"Fuck, yeah." Roman's grin was careless and jaunty again as he pushed himself to sit upright, then rolled off him and grabbed handfuls of tissues to clean them up. "There's nothing like two cocks rubbing. Who *wouldn't* want that?"

"True," Oscar grinned, holding still until he was dry, then glanced around at the room: very comfortable, and almost sparkling compared to the rest of the place, not that he'd gotten a good look yet. This room was homey, down to the writing desk in the corner. Hell, there was a quilt on the bed that almost looked handmade.

Perhaps noticing him looking, Roman pushed himself to stand and gestured around. "This is yours. Bathroom's through there. I better get to bed. You know where the kitchen is, if you need anything."

Before Oscar could invite him to share the bed, Roman strode out the door. Shortly afterward, another shower sounded from somewhere in the house.

Oscar shook his head and lay there, still and warm and confused.

What the hell was that about? And, more importantly, was it going to continue? Or was this it for sleeping together, now that their friends' scrutiny was about to be turned upon them? No doubt Roman was having the same thoughts.

It was really none of their business, except that Oscar knew in the back of his head that their friends were right: their lifestyles just didn't fit, and neither of them were the settling-down type, and… and…

A hundred excuses for why they wouldn't work floated to mind, but every one lost the battle against the satisfied glow deep in his belly when he lay down for sleep, and the smile that just wouldn't leave his lips.

CHAPTER

Five

OSCAR

"Are you *sure* you don't want to figure something else out?"

Oscar couldn't help but laugh at Falcon from his spot on the couch. His best friend had deposited him there and warned him firmly not to move as he packed for him. "You make it sound like Roman's a serial killer or, I don't know, leaves dirty socks around the house."

"Hmm. I haven't asked Blane."

"If he's a serial killer?"

"Or, more importantly, a serial sock-scatterer." Falcon shook his head. "Trust me. It's important."

Oscar laughed. "Is Blane?"

"No, I have him trained to use the basket now," Falcon said with a world-weary sigh. He sat back on his heels and looked around his place, then at both full duffel bags. "Is that it?"

"I think so." Oscar didn't have much physical stuff to bring around with him—he traveled too much, and storing shit at one of his parents' houses was just too much hassle. "Thanks, man."

"No way," Falcon shook his head. "I feel horrible I can't help more. Like, Jesus." His gaze strayed down to Oscar's knee again.

Oscar's chest jolted, and he avoided Falcon's gaze, instead looking around. They hadn't had the discussion yet about what this meant for his future. "I could go for a cup of coffee before we tackle the stairs again, though."

"Stay there. I'll make it." Falcon nearly sprinted to the kitchen counter along one side of the airy studio apartment.

Oscar laughed. "I ain't moving," he promised, raising both hands in a surrender. "Roman told me off enough for trying to stand long enough to cook breakfast."

"That's the other thing." Falcon was back to worrying, his usual smile turned into a frown, brows furrowing together. "He's away half the time, isn't he? Who's going to look after you?"

Oscar turned his hands palms-down and pushed them down slowly. "Breathe. This isn't the first time I've been injured, and it won't be the last. What's *really* worrying you?"

He waited for the answer, and it was quick.

"You and Roman."

"Well," Oscar laughed. He appreciated that Falcon was honest enough to get straight to the point now that he'd asked. "We're adults, hon." When Falcon brought him the coffee, he carefully tugged his friend down to sit next to him. Then, he wrapped his hands around the steaming mug to let it cool off.

Falcon grumbled and looked away. "I know. I just… don't want to see you hurt, and lately…"

Oscar winced. He'd managed to avoid telling Falcon

about him and Jef, but he didn't expect that to last forever. All Falcon knew was that he'd had his heart trampled lately—the inevitable consequences of sleeping or dating within your company. Jef's hot-and-cold moods certainly hadn't stopped him sleeping with the guy.

Falcon bit his lip when Oscar didn't say anything, but he didn't push. He just squeezed Oscar's shoulder. "Whatever makes you happy. That's all I want."

Oscar leaned in to hug him. "I know. But look how things worked out for you and Blane, hm?"

The moment it came out, he knew he'd made a mistake. The gleam in Falcon's eye, barely-restrained teasing, was all too familiar. "Oh?" Falcon commented innocently.

"Shut up," Oscar instantly told him, wagging a finger, but Falcon's grin just spread.

"Is that on the table?"

"No."

"Are you sure?"

"*Yes.*"

"Would you like it to be?" Falcon asked, the tip of his tongue caught between his teeth in mischief.

Oscar swatted his shoulder. "I'm not telling you anything."

"Fine. I see how it is," Falcon grinned, but at least he looked less worried. "Withhold information, why don't you."

"By the time you admitted things were serious, you two were halfway to engaged," Oscar retorted.

"Only because you were so busy on tour—" Falcon broke off, looking guilty.

And here they came to the thornier issue. Oscar sighed, knowing damn well they had to address it outright now, or it would only fester. "I'm out for six to eight weeks. I'll miss this show, and probably the next. And I was about to get…" he trailed off, then waved a hand. "I had a shot at a good thing. That's all. It's not like I've lost everything. My career isn't over."

He repeated Raj's sentiments from the ER waiting room as if doing so would make him believe them more, but it didn't work.

"Good," Falcon said. He rose to his feet and shouldered his duffel bags. "All right, take your time and finish your coffee I'll get these to the car first."

As Oscar watched after him, he came to the sinking realization that Falcon had believed those words about as much as he did. Avoiding the subject was his way of avoiding crushing any hopes Oscar held.

Despite his cheerful words to anyone who asked, hope was growing pretty damn slim.

CHAPTER

Six

ROMAN

"HERE'S TO HAROLD FINALLY FINDING A FUCKING HOBBY."

It wasn't the first toast at the retirement party, nor the most colorful language, but it brought cheers, laughter, and applause to the room.

Harold was one of the longest-serving captains in the airline fleet. He'd been in the Air Force before becoming a commercial pilot. His stories were legendary, as was his devotion to the skies, and his lack of outside skills, hobbies, or even people surrounding him. Hell, he owned a little Cessna of his own that he flew in on his days off.

It was a typical story, but one that made Roman sad when he thought about it. Harold had gone through three wives, each marriage ending in a neat and tidy divorce when she realized she couldn't keep him on the ground for more than a day at a time.

"I don't need a hobby, as long as ol' Betty lets me ride her!" Harold retorted, to more cheers and applause.

Roman tried not to think about that and drank the nonalcoholic fruit punch, ate cheese, and toasted Harold. The burns and compliments grew steadily less clever throughout the night. Above all, he tried to avoid the inevitable one-to-one.

But Harold was making his rounds, steadily more drunk throughout the night, and he eventually found Roman hiding out by the buffet table.

"Feeding that growing stomach, eh?" Harold teased, slapping Roman's back. "Thanks for making it."

"Of course. My pleasure." Roman meant it, too. For all his quirks and his obsession with flight, Harold was a stand-up guy. He was the kind of guy to teach you a few new things on every flight, and let you believe you'd discovered them on your own.

"You got that long-haul spot, didn't you? Great job, kid. You're young for it, too." Harold thought everyone was young, but Roman resisted pointing that out.

"I got lucky that nobody else wanted it." Most pilots his age were resisting settling down and wanted long-haul. Plus, most of the work was in pre-flight preparation, so one long flight was less work in many ways than several return trips in a day. But Roman had waited a long time and impressed enough people to get his chance.

On the other hand…

"And what about your love life, eh? Meet anyone exotic?" Harold gave him a wicked grin. "That's the best part of those long trips. A girl in every port. Or a fellow."

It always took Roman aback how open Harold was to it, but it had only taken one or two half-told military stories before he got the idea: Harold didn't care who did what with whom, as long as they were happy.

Roman looked down for a second. "Yeah, yeah. That's good."

Harold didn't miss a thing. "You doing anything besides work with your life, kid? And that bunch of friends you talked about. Once they all get married off, life gets a lot longer, let me tell you." He was definitely drunk off his ass, but he wasn't about to be stopped, even when Roman tried to press another drink on him. He just took the drink, sipped, and went back to his spiel. "Don't let the fame and money get to your head, kid. Or you'll be staring a lonely retirement in the face. Not that I'm lonely when I've got Betty, ha ha, but I'm not sharing her!"

Roman joined in the good-natured laugh, but there was something in Harold's tone that pricked at his heart. He suddenly felt less like fruit punch and more like wine, or the harder stuff. "I'll remember that."

Harold clapped his arm, gave a few more words of advice, and moved on, but Roman didn't stay much longer. He made his excuses and ducked out within a few minutes, grabbing his coat.

Without thinking about it, he set a course for Blane's house.

"Hey, man." Blane opened the door, and for once, Falcon wasn't hovering over his shoulder. "Come in." He automatically ushered Roman inside.

God, Roman was glad to have him around. *Until he gets married, anyway.* Harold's words were nagging him now. Normally he might have laughed them off, but they must have hit something deeper inside. "Thanks," he said, a little more meaningfully than he meant to.

Blane looked at him quickly. "Of course. You all right? Want a beer?"

"Nah, I gotta drive. I'll take a pop or whatever."

Blane brought out two Cokes and settled on the sofa with him. They spent a few minutes talking about nothing at all—Blane's day at the zoo, Roman's last flight, their plans for the next week.

Finally, Blane broke into Roman's attempt to calm down with non-conversation with a blunt, "What's up? You're not yourself." Roman tried to shrug it off and Blane elbowed him hard.

"Ow. Fucker." It didn't really hurt, but he had to say it anyway.

Blane glared. "That's for brushing me off."

Roman sighed and rubbed his ribs, then shrugged. "I just got back from Harold's retirement party. That's the old guy, the Air Force pilot."

"Yeah, I remember him," Blane nodded, folding his arms and waiting.

Roman fidgeted with his can, pressing his thumbnail into it while he tried to figure out how to say it. "I've been thinking I want a relationship. Is that weird?"

He didn't expect the burst of laughter from Blane, which rolled into even harder laughter when Blane saw the look on his face. "Sorry," Blane managed after a few more seconds, rubbing his face. "I just…" More laughter.

Roman couldn't help but laugh at his best friend's laughter, even if he was vaguely pissed off about not being taken seriously. "What? You don't think I can?"

"No," Blane quickly answered, catching his breath and wiping his eyes. "No, it's just… man. Did you *hear* yourself?"

"What's wrong with wanting that?" Roman's shoulders rose defensively.

Blane slapped his shoulder. "Don't take this the wrong way, but you've been flinging yourself at every guy you've looked at twice since high school. We've talked about this before. How many times have you mentioned marriage on a first date?"

"It's important to know what they think of the future before you... okay," Roman groaned when Blane looked at him pointedly. "Fine. But I'm *happy* with what I've got. A fellow in every port."

Blane's grin faded to a smile as he looked at Roman, his gaze flickering between his eyes. "Are you? Or is that what you say 'cause you keep scaring them off?"

That stung. Roman closed his mouth and looked away for a second, trying not to take it as an insult.

Blane punched his arm gently to get his attention. "Hey. It's not a bad thing. Any port in a storm, to piggyback on your metaphor. Everyone likes fun. Hookups are fun. But I already knew you're the settling-down type. *You* knew that."

Roman looked back at him and nodded, paying attention now. Blane was the type to make fun of him, but only to get through his defenses. "Right..." he trailed off dubiously.

"So slow down a little, and stop trying to plan your garden layout every time you meet a guy. Get to know them as friends first."

"Without sex?" Roman was aghast. The idea of getting to know someone before he even knew if they'd work in bed was so not him.

Blane laughed at his expression again. "Friends with benefits works. Just not, *future husband*, with every guy you stick it in."

Roman snorted and took his turn to elbow Blane, hard. "Not *every* guy." His cheeks burned at the accuracy, though. *I bet he's just been waiting for me to ask. Now that he's with Falcon, and Deen and Nico are together... oh, shit. I'm a project.* "Are you coaching me here?"

"If you don't put yourself out there, I'll make you start running windsprints," Blane cheerily told Roman. "But don't force the romance and you'll be amazed how fast it happens. Just put yourself out there as, like, a friend. The guy *we* see. Not the eligible bachelor seeking same."

"But then you're telling me not to expect what I should be expecting..."

"Don't overthink it," Blane added. "That goes for the romance, too. When it happens, you'll know."

That was about the least useful advice Roman could imagine. He briefly considered punching Blane, then decided to just chug his Coke before he scoffed. "Just like everyone says."

"For real, though." This time, Roman anticipated Blane's kick enough to fend it off. "Don't sit around moping... and don't get so attached to your image as Mr. Slick that you can't see a good thing staring you in the face."

"It's like... I'm going zero or a hundred on the romance," Roman said slowly, and the grin on Blane's face as realization dawned was no less annoying than his laughter earlier. "I guess you're right. Asshole."

Blane laughed. "You're welcome."

"I better get home and make sure Oscar fed himself." Roman pretended not to see the glint in Blane's eye. "See you next weekend? Or the weekend after?"

"I'll make it," Blane promised, clapping him on the shoulder and seeing him to the door. "Keep me posted."

"I will."

It was all Roman could do not to look like he was fleeing, even if he felt like he was.

By the time he got to his house, he felt like he had a plan. He was already doing well with getting to know Oscar as a friend. Maybe they were fucking a little too much for friends, but there were definitely benefits.

So he'd tone back the sex, dial up the friendship, and see what happened. At the very least, he could use more friends, and befriending his near-brother's boyfriend's best friend... as much as it twisted his brain to think of the label... well, that seemed like a good idea.

He burst through the door with a cheery, "Evening!"

Oscar was on the couch watching TV, his leg propped up on the couch. He nearly jumped at the entrance. "Jesus! Someone's in a mood. Party went well?"

Much better than earlier, thank God. Roman just beamed back at him. "Really good. Harold seems happy to retire. He'll be up in that little Cessna every day." When he sat on the couch, Oscar ran his hand up his thigh and back down, less than subtly. It was hard work, but Roman kept his focus. "Have you eaten?"

"Huh?" Oscar blinked. "Oh. No. Just snacks."

"I'll make food."

Oscar looked surprised as Roman stood again. "Are you sure? Are you drunk?"

Roman snorted. "I wouldn't drive drunk. I just went to see Blane, that's all."

"Oh." Oscar brightened. "How's he doing? And Falcon?"

"I didn't ask about the move. Last time I did that, he started muttering about inspections and shit," Roman laughed. "But he seems good. Falcon wasn't there."

"Mm. Must be packing." Oscar hesitated, then tried to stand. "Need a hand with supper?"

"Nope." Roman wagged a finger. "While I'm here, you rest, I'll cook. You'll have time enough to cook when I'm off to London next week."

Leaving town with a man he didn't know very well living in his house felt bizarre, but given the circumstances, not unsafe. Hell, weirdly enough, even if he *hadn't* known Oscar through Blane and Falcon, he'd trust him here. Oscar seemed honest, if overly flirtatious.

He only let Oscar move to the table to eat, then took care of the dishes himself and led him back to the couch for a movie.

And, to Roman's enormous credit, he managed to turn down Oscar when he started rubbing his upper thigh again. He covered Oscar's hand with his own and held hands for a bit, then looped his arm around his shoulders affectionately.

Oscar didn't try again, though he did give Roman a few quizzical looks.

Friendship. By the time Roman headed to his bedroom, he was feeling pretty damn proud of himself. *I didn't fuck him. I mean, benefits are nice, but we can't get to know each other if all we do is fuck.*

By turning down the handjob, he'd already found out tonight what kind of movies Oscar liked, and some of his fond memories of Christmas movies.

I can do this with guys. Start with Oscar. Move on when... when he loses interest. No sweat.

CHAPTER

Seven

OSCAR

THE DAWN LIGHT SPREAD ITS TENDRILS THROUGH THE CRACKS in the blinds like agents of the sun sent to personally harass Oscar.

Normally he didn't mind mornings. He'd even call himself a morning person, he was so accustomed to early rises for rehearsals and travel. But in the last week, his lazy side seemed to have come out.

Stress about the future aside, it was *nice* to have some time off, even if it was enforced by his own body. He didn't have to get up early and go anywhere, or do much of anything. He kept the house tidy around him, but that was about it. Roman wouldn't let him do much of anything, like a mother hen.

Which brought him to the other reason he was so tired —despite going to bed at a reasonable hour, the same time as Roman, he'd stayed awake thinking about his odd behavior.

Maybe it was only one night, the high of a party with coworkers and seeing his best friend, but Roman had turned down a handjob not once, but twice. Oscar wasn't sure how he felt about that.

It wasn't that he felt ugly or scorned—he knew he was hot. Enough guys had told him as much. But something else nagged him, and he couldn't put his thumb on it. He'd given up trying in the small hours of the morning, when his eyes finally grew heavy and tired of staring at the crisp white ceiling.

When he heard Roman cooking breakfast—he seemed to make toast, bacon, and scrambled eggs every morning—Oscar finally got up, too. By the time he'd showered, put his brace on again, and pulled on clothes, then hobbled to the dining room table, breakfast was just about ready.

He couldn't help but wonder if Roman timed the breakfast based on the sounds of him turning off the shower, because those scrambled eggs weren't dried out. They were perfectly fluffy.

"Morning!" Roman greeted from the stove and gave him a cheery smile. "Sleep well?"

"Not as well as I would with you in my bed," Oscar retorted, going for the direct approach. He winked. "You?"

Roman laughed. "Probably the same. But I'd better not get used to anything I'd miss. I'm gonna be away for five more days in your time zone."

Oscar was still working on parsing that. *Something he would miss? Me?* "I… Oh. Yeah, right. Hong Kong again?"

"Yep. A long, boring flight, and then a couple long, boring days in Hong Kong before I head back." Roman sighed at his breakfast. "I used to be glad they put us up in a hotel with good Western breakfasts, but now I don't mind rice for breakfast."

"Rice for breakfast?" Oscar's training regimen was too

strict to allow much rice or carbs at all, except as part of a post-workout recovery meal, so he hadn't eaten the local cuisine since his first international tour.

Roman laughed. "Everyone says that. It's not that bad! It fills you up. Cereal is weird in other countries."

"Cereal is weird in all countries." Oscar nodded at the breakfast. "My trainers would approve of that."

"So would mine," Roman grinned and patted his stomach.

That brought Oscar to something he was curious about. "So, you're kind of… ripped." This was already a little flirtier than the average breakfast conversation. "Do you just spend all your days off in the gym?"

"Actually, no," Roman laughed. "But at least an hour a day, usually. I've explored all the cities I can now. Meeting people in the gym is a good way to find new outdoor spots—running partners, the like—and sometimes drinking buddies who don't mind if you don't drink alcohol."

"Oh!" It was like a lightbulb for Oscar, who usually wasn't allowed alcohol, either. It screwed with his body chemistry too much, and he needed every advantage in muscle recovery to keep from injury.

Not that it did much good, he groused. *Fucking kneecap. Not even in a fucking show. On the street, like a civilian.*

"Yeah," Roman chuckled. "There's a life hack for you."

Oscar cleared his throat. "So, uh, you don't mind me… staying here while you're gone? I can always figure out—"

"Jesus, stop trying to make me kick you out," Roman cut him off with a good-natured laugh. "I know where to find your best friend anyway and shake him down if you make off with the TV. Not that it won't be obvious to the neighbors," he pointed with his fork at Oscar's leg. "You won't make off with anything quickly."

Nobody had made that kind of joke since the injury, so Oscar was torn between horror and amusement, but laughter won. It was kind of... *nice*... not to be handled like fragile glass. "You asshole."

Roman swallowed his sausage and beamed. "Glad to help."

"And, uh... if anyone asks..."

"You're a friend staying here. Tell 'em the truth," Roman said, cheerful as ever, and ignoring his subtler hint.

"Right. A friend."

Roman winked. "Who's had benefits, but most people don't need to know that."

So Roman was definitely not pushing for a relationship. Given what he knew about him—that he jumped into relationships both feet first—Oscar was weirdly almost offended by it, but tried not to be.

Maybe he saw him as more than fucking material. *That* would be nice. Someone who fucked him *and* liked him. His mind went to Jef before he could stop it.

Oscar just nodded back at Roman. "Yeah, let's keep that between us."

There was nothing platonic in the way Roman winked back, sending one more mixed signal into the whole mess he'd presented Oscar with in the last day. "Our dirty little secret."

It wasn't fair that Roman got to say something like that, then jet off to China or Japan or wherever and forget about it. That left Oscar in a place that looked like Roman, smelled like him, was filled with reminders of him.

It was the next day, so by now, the flight had almost landed. Oscar had barely slept again last night, his own attempt at cooking breakfast falling flat compared to yesterday's.

Slowly but surely, the boredom was creeping in. He should have expected it. He didn't know a single athlete who was happy sitting on his ass instead of practicing. A week off was a rare luxury, but as it approached two, and his knee still ached every time he put weight on it, his frustration grew.

Oscar reminded himself for the hundredth time in twenty-four hours that it was probably affecting how he saw this whole thing with Roman.

They'd entered it explicitly agreeing that it was a fling, something to hide from their friends, a friends-with-benefits kind of deal. So there was absolutely no point in moping about that now.

Not that I'm moping. He wasn't falling for the guy or anything—they hardly knew each other, still.

With that decided, Oscar figured he'd try his luck. He opened up his phone, sending Roman another suggestive photo of himself in his underwear. He had that sexual flush in his face and half-lidded eyes.

He added the caption, *Look whose bed you could be in. Shame for you. ;)*

It took an hour or so before he got an answer, but it was worth the wait—what must have been an older picture of Roman in return, his hands barely covering his manhood as he lay on his back on the bed, knees up.

The caption read: *I feel sorry for you missing out on this, too. ;)*

Oscar licked his lips, then responded, *Missing out on what? I can't see the goods...*

Roman sent back a quick *LOL*, and then, *Wait an hour.*

An hour? With my cock this hard? Oscar wasn't actually hard yet, but he was starting to get turned on at the conversation—especially when he thumbed back to the photo.

Half an hour.

Deal.

Twenty-nine minutes after the message, there was another photo—Roman on his back on the bed, looking tussled and tired but with a naughty gleam in his eye, his hand wrapped around his hard cock.

"Whew," Oscar breathed out, squirming off the couch and making for his bedroom. He was going to need some serious alone time with that photo.

When his reaction covered the shower wall, he sent back a photo of it, and he got a photo just as dirty in return.

So nothing much has changed after all. Oscar smiled with relief as he looked back through the day's photos and added them to his jerk-off album.

Their relationship could be light, flirty, sexy, fun, and above all, unnamed. This flirtation and seduction didn't have to affect their living situation.

To be honest, the idea of a sneaky booty call relationship behind their friends' backs made him a little hot. Secretive, but there in plain sight, too.

Besides, Roman was probably right to shut down his not-quite-asked questions about relationships. With this kind of schedule, half of their relationship—if they even tried one—would be Skype calls and photos.

Surely that couldn't work out long-term.

CHAPTER
Eight
ROMAN

THE MIDDLE SHIFT WAS ROMAN'S FAVORITE IN MANY WAYS. Takeoff and landing involved most of the hard work, and the other guys on the deck needed to meet their quotas by handling them this time.

The only problem was the sleeping quarters. In most aircraft he flew, they resembled the overhead cab bed in an RV, they were so compact and the ceiling so low... only instead of one king bed, there were three singles with just curtains as dividers.

It wasn't that he was claustrophobic, exactly, but it set him at ill-ease, especially if he was in the middle. He was glad to scramble out, neaten his uniform, and take over the copilot's job.

Jack was a well-respected captain, and an easy guy to fly with. Long silences weren't awkward, but neither was conversation. He was meticulous with the checklists and monitoring his instruments, and that kind of precision made Roman relax.

"You've been doing long-haul flights your whole career?"

Roman finally asked, after a few minutes admiring the Atlantic silently together.

"Just about. Once I was made captain, they happened to need someone who didn't mind being away from home a week at a time. A lot of the guys with young kids didn't want it," Jack answered, settling back in his seat and looking over at him. "Why? Are you second-guessing your choice to join our weary crew?"

Roman laughed. "Not exactly. Well, I guess. It just gets… claustrophobic after a while. And I don't mind the stretches abroad, but being home more often would be nice."

"You're settling down." Jack raised an eyebrow. "Found yourself going steady?"

The antiquated phrase made Roman smile even more. "Nah. I mean, not yet." He drummed his fingers on his knee, looking at his flight instruments to avoid making eye contact. "I thought I wanted to see the world. And I have seen a bit of it… but I don't know."

"A white picket fence is sounding better?" Jack guessed.

Roman nodded. "Yeah. I think Harold got to me," he admitted with a laugh. "He was nagging me about not letting life pass me by. And I know I'm one of the youngest on the roster, but I feel too old for partying in Hong Kong half the week, then quiet little Knoxville the other half."

"It's a big adjustment." Jack looked at him thoughtfully, then folded his arms. "Well, if I were you, I'd think closely before I ditched this and went back to short-haul. You were lucky to grab this spot. And life at home is different, especially if you've got someone waiting there."

Roman did now, in a way. Already he was worrying about things like whether he'd have enough time at home to rake the leaves, since Oscar certainly couldn't, or if he should have left more meals in the fridge for him.

Short-haul was more tiring in many ways, being up and down all the time and flying a couple flights per day. What if it didn't have the sex appeal and glamor of a long-haul pilot? Surely Oscar—*men*, he reminded himself firmly, as in the generic men he might be interested in dating—wouldn't mind. A pilot was a pilot to them, unless he had enough stripes to be even sexier.

"You're right," Roman nodded slowly. "But they would let me transfer back, huh?"

"There's no shortage of guys who want your job," Jack told him and slapped his knee. "It's not a bad thing. We've all got different preferences, and we move around in different stages of life, you know? When my kid got sick, I stuck to the continent so I could be around more. But they won't look kindly on you switching back again for another few years, so make sure it's what you want."

Roman sighed under his breath. He wasn't even sure what he wanted, or whether this was a hare-brained idea. At least now, he had long stretches of days off, so he'd been able to get Oscar settled in before taking off again.

I'm not going to do anything hasty, he decided. Way too soon for that. He and Oscar weren't even officially… anything. He hadn't even let Oscar get that close when he'd hinted around it. No sense, when he'd only chase him off and screw up everything good about his life in the process.

"And if this something you really want to do, don't let petty shit get in the way," Jack added meaningfully.

Jesus. If he's talking about Cory, he must have heard something. And who else knows? Everyone? Roman's cheeks burned. He glanced sideways at Jack, then nodded. "Thanks, man," he finally answered and changed the subject to sports, letting Jack fill him in on the latest college football.

The decision left unmade sat heavily in Roman's chest. He was going to need a sounding board for this, and that meant one thing: his significant brothers.

CHAPTER
Nine

OSCAR

PAYING FOR AN UBER WAS TOTALLY WORTH IT FOR BRUNCH. No way was Oscar missing their biweekly tradition, especially when he had few other means of staying in touch with his colleagues and friends right now.

"Look who the cat dragged in!" one of his friends, Matt, exclaimed.

Oscar laughed and pulled over a chair next to him, squeezing in so he didn't have to take the empty chair next to Jef. "Nice to see you too, jerk."

"Oh! Yeah, how's the leg? They have to cut it off?" Matt grinned.

Oscar rolled his eyes. "Don't strain your sympathy muscle."

"I've only got one, and it just got engaged, you know." Matt had done a flashdance proposal to his boyfriend, which Oscar, among the others, had helped with.

"Incapable of sympathy except in exchange for sexual favors," Oscar pretended to note down. "Sounds about right.

The leg's all right. Not gonna be dancing anytime soon, but the kneecap hasn't budged."

Raj leaned over the table to listen in, but didn't comment —he just returned to whatever conversation he was engaged in when Oscar finished.

"And you guys?" Oscar made himself ask, pushing through the moment of jealousy.

"I need to get hungover more often. That turn I was having so much trouble with? It's easy when I just relax."

"I told you that," Oscar said and laughed. "Everyone did."

"Yeah, but it took me giving zero fucks about anything and not putting effort in to actually realize I was overdoing it," Matt told him. "Guess what? It looks a lot better now."

Oscar wondered who had taken his spot in the choreography, or if they'd re-blocked anything. *Thinking that way doesn't do any good, though,* he reminded himself. *It just leads to heartbreak.* "All on track?"

"As much as we ever are." Matt waved a menu at him. "Staying for brunch?"

"Wait, you were hungover?"

"The club crawl Friday night," Matt said, as if it were obvious. It was the first Oscar had heard of it, though. "I had thirteen beers."

"Jesus Christ. That's taking cheat day to a new level."

Matt toasted that with his glass of water while Oscar paged through the menu. Oscar's sole consolation was that he got to eat as much as he damn well wanted for a few more weeks, especially if it would speed up recovery. Sugary breakfast syrups were in fashion; vegetables arranged to look tasty were so last month.

Why hadn't they invited him out? Was he the lame duck now?

The words sat harshly on his mind, making him twist his fingers together. Most of the guys knew better, but some people thought like that without even realizing what they were doing—socially isolating him.

It wasn't like he could dance or club, though. He'd just have been stranded on a barstool watching everyone else have fun. Maybe they were right not to invite him.

Definitely right, if you're gonna keep moping like this, the thought occurred to him.

Instead, Oscar made himself smile. "Is there photo evidence?"

"Is there ever!"

Some people protested, but the photos and videos were passed around anyway. It looked like everyone had had a blast on their evening out without him, which didn't make the uncomfortably jealous feelings subside one bit.

There was Jef, the dick, dancing without a care in the world. *He* wouldn't step off a stage at an inconvenient moment and twist a knee.

Okay, now you're getting ugly. Oscar just laughed at the videos and passed back Matt's phone. "How you filmed all that drunk off your ass, we'll never know."

"Long practice."

"Hear, hear."

They subsided into discussions about tweaks Raj was making to their practice routine today, which was no less exclusionary a subject than their fun weekend out.

Oscar was just starting to regret coming when the waiter showed up to take their orders.

Mercifully, Matt asked him about Falcon's art, which gave Oscar a chance to brag about his best friend for a while, and segued into a discussion of different art styles.

"I still think photorealistic paintings take more skill. I mean, you're trying to fool the human eye. That's like, the most powerful machine there is," Jess exclaimed.

"Yeah, but to figure out how to condense a whole bunch of detail into one daub?" Oscar argued, just for the spirited discussion.

Jess waved a hand but grinned at him. "Fine. I'll let it drop, but I don't agree."

This was a little more like the usual. Good old times. Sitting around, picking at the remains of carefully-ordered breakfasts with a million substitutions, talking about nothing important while they waited to go to practice…

Ugh. He'd just head home. There was no point in sitting around watching everyone else do things he couldn't.

And it would be home to an empty house, which brought his mood down again. He sent a quick group text with his address and said out loud, "I just sent a group text, y'all. My address."

"In case we want to stalk you?" Jef's grin brought laughter, but privately, it was disconcerting. He didn't think anyone else had noticed the weird dynamic between them.

"Or visit me and bring flowers, whatever."

Matt scowled. "You don't have a cast to sign, though."

"You can Sharpie on my knee instead," he offered.

"Deal."

Jef was frowning to himself at his phone, but Oscar didn't even try to guess what was going through his mind. He didn't care.

Jef announced, "Time to head out soon, guys. With Raj around, we can't even pretend we got lost."

They laughed as they settled their bills. The place was close enough to the studio that everyone could walk there—

everyone with functional legs, of course. Oscar opened his phone app to call another taxi.

Matt lingered by him for a moment. "Want me to wait?"

"I'm not gonna fall over without support," Oscar laughed and waved him on, but he felt better with one person, at least, giving a shit. "Thanks, though."

He was glad when the last of them had disappeared around the corner, so he could let his smile drop. Even waiting outside here, alone, was lonelier than he'd expected. He was jazzed up, filled with energy his body fully expected to burn in a long practice session. And now he just felt empty, without anyone to banter or laugh with about stupid, random shit.

Maybe brunch wasn't such a good idea.

The Uber driver seemed surprised that he leaned forward to make conversation, but soon gladly started talking about his most interesting rides lately, giving Oscar a few laughs and distracting him.

At least, until he dropped him off, and Oscar remembered he had a few more days before Roman even got back.

They hardly used group texts right now—this was their equivalent of shore leave, being back in their hometown for a few weeks before taking off for the next tour. And after they left without him? Not a chance he could get through to them. Road life was crazy.

Maintaining friendships was gonna be damn hard. Not for the first time, Oscar wished he could take back that single second of his life—the split-second of distraction that had cost him so dearly.

But wishes get you nowhere, he reminded himself and limped inside for an afternoon nap to sleep off that stack of pancakes. *And at least I'm free for now.*

Free to do nothing but twiddle his thumbs.

Ten

ROMAN

"You all knew you were gay by, what, tenth grade?"

The guys looked at each other with a laugh. "Or bi, or whatever," Josh answered Oscar with a wave of his hand. "Anyway, we kind of accidentally found each other before we were out. But we all came out around the same time."

"Safer that way," Dustin said.

Roman met Blane's glance with one of his own. They were both remembering Dustin back then, the scrawny nerd in the group, as he still was today. He'd certainly been safer around them than most of their Tennessee classmates a decade ago.

Very few kids dared pick on the guys built like a brick outhouse: Roman, Blane, Josh, Nico, and Tyler. Give or take fifty pounds and a few inches, they'd looked like an evenly-matched football offensive line compared to most high schoolers.

Even today, they weren't small guys. Roman hung out in the gym, Blane lifted heavy animals at the zoo, Josh owned a dude ranch, and Nico was a park ranger in the Smokies.

Tyler was lighter than the rest of them now, a deliberate choice for a driver, but kept the muscle tone he could without gaining too much weight.

Dustin, now a forensics geek, had always been the one squeezed into the middle seat of the car, or the one they boosted through an open window when someone forgot his house key.

"I bet," Oscar answered, glancing around at them. "And… significant brothers?"

"Ah, I was just getting to that part," Josh laughed.

The story never got old: turned away from a high school prom for going without girls as *significant others*, they'd come up with the retort, "What about significant brothers?" The name had stuck.

Oscar was just as delighted to hear the story behind the name as Deen and Falcon had been, not too long ago on either count. "That's awesome. I wish I'd gone to your school."

"Next round's mine," Roman announced, to the delight of the rest of them. He took orders and headed to the bar.

Oscar trotted to catch up to him. "You'll need a hand or two carrying all that."

Roman grinned and slowed down, almost reaching out to put a hand on his back before he remembered where they were. "Yeah. Thanks."

"So, when did you know?" Oscar piped up.

Roman smiled at Oscar's fascination. "That I'm gay? Oh, early on. My parents thought so but weren't really sure. They only knew the Will & Grace kind of gays, you know?" he chuckled.

Oscar grinned. "You weren't the high-heels type? I was. Mom loved it."

From his choice of words when they'd talked about Oscar getting the rest of his stuff from his parents, and this phrase, Roman could guess his dad hadn't been a fan. "Your parents weren't together?" he questioned instead, carefully.

"Back then they were. They split when I was seventeen," Oscar told him with a careless shrug.

"Sorry."

"It's fine. They're happier this way," Oscar insisted. "When I went off to the conservatory, I think it gave them the chance."

Roman nodded, rubbing Oscar's shoulder before he was even conscious he was doing it. "Mine are together, just outside Nashville. Boring suburban family. I don't talk to them a lot. Growing up is weird."

"I know," Oscar agreed. "I'm kinda glad I don't have to. Except Mom. I email her once in a while, and she comes to performances if they're in Tennessee. That's about it. She's pretty busy with her own business."

"Oh, that's neat." Not for the first time, Roman felt staid in comparison—standard middle-class guy with a pretty tame, if slightly inconvenient, job, and a couple married parents who held office jobs. "Think you got some of that independent spark from her? Ever planning to settle down?"

"Probably," Oscar smiled. "Settling down doesn't seem so bad sometimes. Boring right now, but that's because I can't *do* anything."

Roman patted his back and looked at the bar. The service was damn slow tonight. Then, he realized they were at the service end and nudged Oscar with a laugh. "We'd better get around the corner to get served."

Oscar realized their mistake, too, and laughed. "Easy to get caught up..." he trailed off.

Just talking to each other, I forget the rest of the world's around. Roman felt a dizzying rush of realization but pushed it away and strode around the corner of the bar, squeezing between two empty bar stools.

Oscar joined him in the narrow space, leaning on the counter but close enough their thighs touched. It distracted Roman enough that he missed what Oscar said, and had to replay it in the part of his brain that was used to storing and dealing with transmissions from air traffic control and other pilots.

Something about how often we do this? "Oh, every week or two if we can. Less often if we're busy. It's pretty flexible. Usually not all of us can make it—mostly me." Roman chuckled. "But you could come along pretty much anytime if you wanted. Might keep you busy while I'm away. If you wanted."

Oscar relaxed, shooting Roman a grateful look.

"You're that bored you wanna hang out with us?" Roman grinned.

"My colleagues from the company… aren't really staying in touch," Oscar said, then flagged down the bartender for their order.

With that, they didn't have a chance to continue the conversation, but the comment lingered on Roman's mind as he and Oscar took turns carrying the round of drinks back to the table.

Oscar had insisted on calling them an Uber each way and Roman was allowed to drink tonight, so he enjoyed a few beers that much more.

Maybe some of the extra enjoyment came from having Oscar pressed into his side in the booth, his hand sometimes resting on Roman's knee. Oscar flirted and laughed and joked, but the tension between them was growing harder to ignore.

It was no easier watching Nico and Deen kiss or Falcon touch Blane's back affectionately. Roman almost ached to do the same with Oscar, but they weren't there yet. If ever.

But there was no way he could resist Oscar tonight, blossoming friendship or not, and judging by Oscar playing footsie under the table, he was feeling about the same. When they finally rose to leave, Blane caught his eye. Roman pretended not to see the questioning look.

"We better get going. I have some stuff to do tomorrow before I'm Europe-bound," Roman excused himself, leaning in for back-pats and half-hugs and handshakes around the table.

The Uber arrived mercifully quickly, but the evening wasn't so cold it could justify how close they stood as they waited.

"That was fun. Your friends—brothers—are great," Oscar told Roman, leaning into him.

"I know. They like you, too." Roman wrapped an arm around his waist for a moment. When he reluctantly dropped it, Oscar turned, picked up his hand, and pirouetted to wrap himself in Roman's arm again, draping it over his shoulder. Roman laughed and didn't resist. "Bold little thing, aren't you?"

"Little?" Oscar challenged with a grin. "You know better."

"You *are* all muscle," Roman amended, then let his gaze flicker down. "And other things."

The black car pulled up before Oscar could say anything, but he flicked his tongue out for a moment before he ducked into it.

Little twerp. Roman slid in beside him and buckled up

automatically. Oscar's hand found his in the darkness between the seats, and they played with each other's fingers and palms on the drive home.

The impatience was an inferno under Roman's skin now, making him fumble to get his keys in the door when they *finally* reached his house.

"Distracted?" Oscar teased, running his hand up Roman's arm to his shoulder and rubbing the back of his neck.

Roman tried to slap away Oscar's hand with a laugh. "Give me five seconds."

"No. I want you now," Oscar said simply, and this time, his hand ran from the back of Roman's neck down his spine, slowly, toward the curve of his back and his ass.

Roman almost fell through the front door as it opened, pulling Oscar after him.

They barely made it to the couch. Roman led the way, more certain in the dark, steering Oscar by the hand. When he sat, he pulled Oscar down sharply to sit next to him and they collapsed together, laughing.

With his eyes adjusting already, it was easy to see the curve of Oscar's smile in the semi-dark. Roman's gaze lingered on it, and then he leaned in, curling his hand around the back of Oscar's head and pulling him in for a slow kiss.

They kissed like it was their first time exploring this sharp-edged new thing together. Even if it was a familiar tension between them by now, it felt strange, perhaps because it was continuing now when it usually didn't last past one night.

"Since you've invited me in, I should return the favor." Oscar's smirk was nearly audible.

"Slick, aren't you?" Roman teased.

"Takes one to know one." Oscar's hand found his in the darkness, their fingers lacing tightly.

Roman grinned. "My brothers called me Mr. Slick. Still do sometimes." It was weird, too, that he hadn't been able to find cheesy pickup lines or smooth tricks to get what he wanted. He didn't have to. It just seemed to naturally *happen*.

"Convenient. I want you leaving me slick," Oscar whispered.

Enough of this thinking shit. He leaned in to kiss Oscar again—harder, this time. Oscar melted into him, sliding an arm around his shoulders. His other hand crept up Roman's thigh as he walked his fingers up. Every press of Oscar's fingertip against skin made him tingle, even if there were too many clothes in the way.

There was a sharp intake of breath as Oscar felt how hard he was just from kissing him and being so close. Then, Oscar grinned against his mouth and nipped his lower lip. He didn't say anything, but he slowly pulled down the zipper.

Roman fumbled for Oscar's pants to return the favor, pressing feverish kisses until they were gasping for breath into each other's mouths.

Carefully, they helped each other pull their pants down, hands wrapped around hardening flesh. Their bodies crushed close together in the darkness, they panted into each other's mouths.

Still, neither of them said anything, following pure instinct. On Roman's part, at least, he felt like saying anything might break this moment between them.

Oscar squeezed him tightly and Roman shivered with the desire building under his skin, thrusting his hips up into Oscar's tight hand. It took all his focus to keep caressing Oscar in return. Rubbing his palm over the head, twisting his hand on the upstroke, made Oscar's hips jerk up off the couch, and he made a mental note of that.

Conscious thought slipped away as Roman pressed closer to Oscar, rubbing the heads of their sensitive shafts together.

Still silent except for quiet gasps and stifled moans, they finished one at a time, leaving the sticky evidence of their passion streaked across both of their stomachs as they shifted their hands to each other's hips and sides instead.

Roman pressed his forehead against Oscar's, shivering at the hot breaths across his cheek as Oscar caught his breath. Still, he didn't say anything as his brain kicked in again.

That wasn't very platonic.

The itch under his skin to hold Oscar close that night was far more disconcerting than any other attraction to him could be. Roman finally let go of Oscar, pressing one more kiss against his lips.

He really had to get his ass to bed before he said something he'd regret. Roman pushed away slowly from Oscar to stand up, grabbing handfuls of tissues to clean himself up and pushing some into Oscar's hand.

Roman couldn't see Oscar's expression well in the dark, but he didn't seem surprised when Roman raised a hand and stumbled for his room and bed.

It was the right thing to do. He wasn't going to try to romance a guy who didn't want his attention, and had every reason to think of him as someone who'd just break his heart. It was better to let Oscar find a man who could be what he needed.

I'd never be that guy. For all Roman knew, he *would* break Oscar's heart if he tried to build some kind of relationship with him.

The word lingered in his mind for a long time as he tried to drift to sleep: *relationship*.

Blane was dead on, as always. It was easy to stifle his own feelings with others around, to hide his desire for a white picket fence and a dog and a boyfriend who made dinner when he came home from work behind his love of sex… but it was a lot harder to lie to himself when he was alone in the dark, waiting for sleep.

What if he could have it all?

CHAPTER
Eleven

OSCAR

"You must be bored shitless."

Oscar couldn't deny it. It felt like he'd been trapped on his own for weeks, even if it had only been two days since Roman left.

But what a hell of a couple days.

Roman was still blowing hot and cold, coming on to him and then acting like buddies the next morning. Oscar wasn't sure exactly what the hell was going on with him, and thinking about it made his head hurt. Especially when he couldn't *do* anything, just wait for Roman to say something more clear than a muddy farm track.

He wasn't gonna be able to relax until Roman was home and dry.

Maybe it was that weakness that made him say yes when Jef texted to say he was coming over to hang out. Not that Jef *asked*, exactly; he assumed and then swanned his way in, as he did in all of life. Oscar had to admit it had worked just fine for him in life thus far.

"Out of my mind," Oscar agreed, fidgeting with his hair as he leaned back on the couch. Jef had insisted on bringing them both water and snacks so Oscar didn't have to move, but the snacks he chose were all high-sugar. "They're letting you eat this stuff?"

Jef laughed under his breath and joined him, passing over the fruit roll-ups. "Not a chance. They're for you."

"How sweet."

"I have my moments." Jef grinned at him and joined him on the couch, a decision that didn't go unnoticed by Oscar.

Are we... what the hell are *we doing?*

Oscar never quite wanted to ask, though. Especially now, when Jef was recounting the stories he was missing, like practice gone awry one day when Ty had a wardrobe malfunction and caught a contagious fit of the giggles.

Most of his life went—or had gone, until now—into this career. It wasn't until he saw the dance-shaped hole in his life that he realized how dangerous that was.

Maybe Raj was right.

The worst part was how quickly he seemed to have fallen out with his former coworkers—a group of men who he counted as his best friends, confidantes, competitors, and co-creators, at different times and in different ways.

It had happened before, when he thought about it. When someone got cut, he'd been appropriately sad, said goodbye like everyone else, and then... kept moving, kept dancing, while someone else's world stopped.

Now that *he* was the one stopping, watching everyone pull out of reach, and nobody looked back at him, he regretted for a moment some of those partings.

"What's on your mind?" Jef said lightly.

Oscar wasn't going to bring down the mood, and the part of him that still viewed Jef as competition—even if he'd won, a fact that bitterly stung if he lingered on it—didn't want to give him the satisfaction. "What I'll make for dinner when Roman comes back."

"Oh, you're a househusband too!" Jef grinned. Somehow, this conversation direction wasn't better.

Oscar eyed him and rolled his eyes. "Never. Can you see me cooking?"

"King of the road ramen."

Despite himself, Oscar laughed.

They'd once been given a cheat day on their diets while acclimatizing to jet lag after landing in the Midwest, but their motel was so far out of town that nobody wanted to grab a taxi into town. Instead, they'd picked up cheap ramen from the corner store, and he'd turned his coffee machine into a ramen maker for everyone.

The memory was another kick in the gut as he played with the gummy bears in his hand, squishing them together until they stuck, then prying them apart.

At least he's here, trying to make me laugh. It's not his fault I'm losing everything.

Oscar forced a smile onto his face. Maybe Jef liked him when he wasn't competition. Better than the rest of the company, ignoring him when he was right here in town with them.

When Jef slid his hand up Oscar's thigh, he wasn't even surprised. He turned his head to study his expression, raising an eyebrow.

"Shame it's not your arm."

"What?"

"So I could do some pickup line about giving you a hand," Jef snickered. "Oh. Was that insensitive?"

Oscar rolled his eyes and resisted the urge to laugh. Yeah, to say the least, but Jef didn't really care what he said now. Experience had taught him that. "Whatever, man. What are we doing?"

"What do you want us to do?" Jef slipped his hand under Oscar's thigh, his other hand going behind his back. Before Oscar could react, he stood, sweeping him off his feet and into his arms.

"How chivalrous," Oscar dryly remarked. Being cradled against a man's chest felt right, but this man? No. There were no butterflies, no barely-concealed grins. There hadn't ever been between them.

"Which way is your room?"

Oscar pointed, wrapping his hand around Jef's shoulder.

It felt wrong—too angular, too sleek and lithe. A fellow dancer's body, not...

Not Roman.

Fuck off, he told himself. *He's not giving you anything. He's giving you 'let's be friends' and 'stay at my place' and then going hot-and-cold.*

Roman wasn't there, and Oscar wasn't sure he ever would be. What surprised him was not that; what surprised him was that *he* was thinking about something more than a fling with a buddy. And Roman. And those two things together.

His brain was short-circuiting. By the time Jef crawled over him on the bed, Oscar shifted uncomfortably.

He'd never fucked a guy while thinking about another guy before. He had the sneaking suspicion that if he tried sleeping with Jef, he was going to have that experience for the first time.

Which made him uncomfortable.

And sex wasn't something that made him uncomfortable —or something he overthought, and his brain had spun through all these thoughts at ninety miles per hour.

"Whoa," Oscar breathed as Jef straddled him, unbuttoning his shirt in swift, efficient movements. He winced when Jef settled back onto his thigh, his knee angled wrong. "Ow."

Jef shifted his weight off him and frowned. "Sorry," he murmured, running his hand up Oscar's stomach. "I'll make it up to you."

Will you, though?

Oscar's heart pounded as Jef unbuttoned his shirt, one at a time. The tease, the anticipation, was good. It wouldn't last long, but it was hot. Right? This was hot. He was supposed to find it hot. Why didn't he?

Oscar's uncertainty prickled into annoyance, then anger, as emotion welled under his skin.

Was he a victory prize for the taking? The star role, and now the man who he'd beat to get it? And not even fair and square. Was this his way of "winning" against Oscar?

He grabbed Jef by the shoulders and pulled him down for a kiss. Just as he'd thought, Jef angled his head away and Oscar tensed up. It wasn't attraction, really. So what the fuck was this, between them?

Was it because he was injured? Was this a pity fuck? He couldn't stand that idea.

And all of this in Roman's house and bed? He made it clear I'm not trading sex for shelter, or even romance... but... it just feels wrong.

The problem kept shifting. He couldn't put his finger on *why* this felt so wrong between them—whether it was because it was Jef, or because he was hung up on Roman, or because he had some crazy self-image issues of his own now that he'd screwed up his leg and felt like a useless lump…

Oscar choked back a gasp when Jef touched his bare chest at last, and he pushed Jef's hand away. "No."

Jef sat back slowly, his expression startled, then wary. "What? You want the lights off or what? We've done it before. I won't freak out if you can't bend into a pretzel tonight."

"It's not that. It just hurts. It's distracting," Oscar mumbled, averting his gaze. The excuse came out all wrong even as he said it. His cheeks burned.

He might sleep around, but he was always honest about it. If he didn't plan to see a guy again, he said it outright and upfront. Lying about why he wanted Jef to leave was…

Well, necessary, because he couldn't tell Jef. *He* didn't even know why yet.

The anger that still sizzled deep in his gut wanted Jef gone, because he was a reminder of what Oscar had lost, *and* the rivalry between them, *and* how much of a dick Jef had been in the past. Wasn't that enough reason?

Jef took a deep breath and swung himself off the bed, not being careful of Oscar's leg. The jostle made Oscar bite his tongue, but he didn't let his expression shift.

"Yeah, right. You're a dancer. You work through the pain, you can fuck through it." Jef buttoned up his own shirt, his eyes dark with anger.

"I don't want to."

"Yeah. You said so." Jef left, and Oscar listened for the thump of the front door slamming. It came a minute later, leaving him alone in the house again.

Oscar let out his breath in a long sigh and rolled his head

back on the pillow. He still smelled Jef's cologne on his own shirt, still felt the phantom warmth of a hand on his thigh.

Of someone who wanted him, even if he wasn't sure how, and even if he didn't want Jef in return.

The thought he was really afraid of came next: *But is Roman any better?*

As long as Roman was dancing around the question of them, he wasn't getting any satisfaction from him, either.

"How the fuck is my life a soap opera?" Oscar pulled a pillow to cover his face and groaned into it, then propped himself up awkwardly so he could punch it a few times. "Fuck you, fuck you, *fuck you.*"

Jef didn't care about him—that much was clear. He'd torn out of here like a bat out of hell. So it *had* been some weird revenge or victory sex, or pity sex, or… something that Oscar didn't want. So they were well and truly done.

That took him out of the picture, leaving Oscar alone with… just Roman.

He had to allow for the possibility of some hypothetical man who might see him and sweep him off his feet and offer him a place to live and cook delicious food, but *not* run away the second feelings were possible.

Oscar lay back down slowly, pressing his cheek to the cool fabric, as it sank in for good: he didn't want that other imaginary guy, even if he existed.

He wanted Roman. And his heart was involved now. And he'd probably felt cold toward Jef because of those… *feelings*… he had for Roman.

I don't do feelings. I've always said I don't do feelings. I want him, and I don't do this. And I don't want to fuck anyone else to take away the sting, and that's a new one for me. Oh, Christ. What the fuck do I do now?

He groaned in a loud, long grunt, then pulled the covers over himself and rolled into a burrito of blankets and his own self-pity. He was fucked—or, quite possibly, not going to be fucked for a long time.

It was up to Roman.

CHAPTER
Twelve

ROMAN

"Shinjuku? Ni-chome? That's, like, two, isn't it? Ichi, ni, san."

Roman was impressed despite himself. He hadn't expected Cory to be able to count to three in any other language. Then again, he hadn't expected Cory to ask where the gay bars were in Tokyo, either.

"You know Japanese? I wouldn't have thought," he bantered lightly, resisting the urge to fidget. He always felt boxed-in when he sat in the backseat of a car. The airport hotel shuttle was somewhat better, being a van, but the seats still felt too efficient for a North American to fit into.

Cory rolled his eyes. "Ha ha. The girls here love an all-American man. I know enough to get through the basics. Ichi, ni, san... hnnh!" He mimed thrusting his hips forward and up. Mercifully, the seatbelt stopped him mid-deflowering.

Roman pulled a face and snorted. "Classy as always."

"What? Don't the guys want to ride a little white lightning?"

Caught between suspicion of Cory's sudden interest and amusement, Roman just shrugged. "Sure."

"What the hell, man. I'm bored, and gay people know how to party. Show me where your people go." Cory clapped his shoulder, seemingly unaware of how loud he was in the confined space of the van. Rude enough in North America, let alone here.

Roman hardly knew what to say. *Maybe he's trying to come around. Maybe someone had a word with him. I gotta give him the benefit of the doubt.* He resisted the urge to sigh, and instead forced a smile. "Yeah, sure. It'll be great." *Like a hole in the head.* "Just don't say anything that gets *me* kicked out, yeah?"

"Come on, man. I would never." Cory launched into a ramble about his last drunken exploits in some exciting bar full of young women who dressed as nurses, and Roman was safe to tune him out for the rest of the drive.

<hr>

As if today weren't already weird enough, Cory didn't freak out and bolt out the door of the first club Roman brought him to. Roman had promised himself he'd give Cory a chance for the first fifteen minutes. In that time, Cory actually seemed to be behaving himself.

He'd hung out with guys who wouldn't even walk in the front door, so despite Cory's previous attitudes, Roman was willing to give him a chance.

Maybe *because* of that attitude. Everyone knew homophobes often wound up being gay, desperate for someone to see through their charade while terrified of it at the same time. On the off-chance Cory needed to see that it was normal as hell, Roman was sticking his neck out.

It made Roman uncomfortable that gay guys suffering internalized homophobia were seen as a joke by most people, like a fitting punishment of the worst possible kind, instead of a tragic, screwed-up, dark thread choking his whole tightly-knit community.

If he hadn't had his buddies by his side back in high school, god only knew where he would have ended up. Maybe laughing at limp-wristed TV caricatures like plenty of the other Knoxville boys his age, afraid of admitting what he was just realizing.

"They make the drinks strong here," Cory whistled, drawing his attention away from his drink and back to him. He was out to have fun, not fix the damn world.

If he didn't know better, he could have sworn Cory was flirting with him. He swiveled back and forth on his bar stool, pushing his drink around on the bar top.

Roman wasn't sure how to treat Cory. From the surprise of even wanting to come here to hitting on him, what the fuck had gotten into him today?

Then a guy wandered past, shooting Roman a regretful look on the way by.

He's cockblocking me. Which made about as much sense as the rest of it. Surprisingly, he didn't mind, since he was in the middle of... whatever this was with Oscar. Roman sighed and shot the rest of his whisky. "What's up?"

"What do you mean what's up?" Cory grinned at him, sipping his whisky slower. "I'm just liking watching actual dancing. I knew the gays were good for something."

Roman nearly banged his head on the bar as he waved for another drink. He was going to need several stiff ones to deal with this. "I mean, you suddenly wanting to come here."

"Just, how the other half lives, you know?" Cory gestured

around. "Where you come after a long flight. Everyone seems friendly here."

Roman bit back his laugh. For the most part, they were, but he could picture Cory wading into drama without ever seeing it coming. By now, he had a few familiar haunts at the end of every long-haul route, and he was a known face there, too.

And, more importantly, he knew which bartenders had jealous boyfriends. Like the one watching Yu serving an awfully handsy twink with an Aussie accent. There was trouble brewing. Better wander down the block to his other favorite place soon.

"Sure. Big happy family."

Cory didn't notice his sarcasm. "And at least they don't cheat you on the drinks. They're *cheap*, man. I'd come here more if I weren't worried about, you know, dropping the soap."

It was all Roman could do not to roll his eyes. *Same old Cory. If he* is *having some identity crisis, he sure as hell ain't admitting it here.* "Whatever, man. I'm pretty tired. I better get back before the trains stop."

"I'm not staying here alone," Cory almost yelped, scrambling to his feet. "I'm fresh blood."

"You're not that hot," Roman shot back, unable to resist.

"And they're into me, man. It's the blue eyes."

Roman couldn't leave fast enough, pursued hotly by Cory. He led the way out of the twisting maze of alleys, past the adult shops that made Cory stumble to a halt and stare for a second at the gay magazines and leather straps framed by the light spilling from the tiny places' windows.

He was tempted to turn right around and have another

few beers, but if he took a drink every time Cory said some-thing stupid, it would take more than the two days they had in Japan to sober up. If he didn't give himself alcohol poisoning.

No, he could cope a healthier way, once he got them back to their fucking hotel.

An hour on the train felt like a year with Cory saying stupid shit about older guys he'd seen trying to pick up pretty young boys, and wondering out loud if gay men had less trouble dating because they were all equally likely to have wandering eyes.

By the time they got to the hotel, Roman barely said good night before he was off to his room, not even waiting for the elevator. He took the goddamn stairs, and he would have paid money to do it.

The burn in his thighs and lungs by the time he got to the fourth floor was totally worth it, but trying to work off the anger only brought more up. Why hadn't he said more back to Cory? Or reported him before now? How long was Cory going to use things he'd said or seen against him at work now?

Roman changed into shorts and a t-shirt and found his way to the gym instead, one of his preferred methods for burning off the alcohol calories and coping with long stretches away from home. Gym equipment was pretty universal—minor details like kilos or pounds aside.

He was able to forget Cory for long enough to work through his routine, focusing all of his attention on not dropping a weight like a drunk dumbass. He hadn't even had that much, but some of the dizziness he felt was probably jet lag.

"Moron," he muttered at last, dropping the barbells on the floor and stretching out on the bench. He hadn't noticed the sweat running down his spine until then, but the wet t-shirt stuck to him. He shuddered and groaned. "God."

He could probably grab a train back to Tokyo if he really wanted time with "his people" without an asshole coworker lording it over him, but... this wasn't what he wanted. None of it was.

For the first time since his first visit, Japan felt too big, too foreign, and he was homesick. He wanted a little town where the waiters at the pizza place knew his name, a house he could stay in longer than a few days...

And Oscar. This was about him, wasn't it?

The realization made him so uncomfortable he slid to the floor to do a few more pushups until failure, but he couldn't avoid it. When he finally hauled himself to sit upright, leaning on the bench, it was as certain in his mind as if he'd read it in a book.

He wanted Oscar. Whatever the fuck was between them, he was tired of putting a label on it, and then worrying whether it was the right one, and what the next label was supposed to be...

Why not just take it as it came, without worrying if they were husband material? There was clearly *something* there.

He pulled his phone out, then perked up. Nearly midnight here meant it was a decent hour back home.

The phone was ringing before he even thought twice.

"Hello?" It was Oscar's voice, warm and familiar, and suddenly Roman wanted nothing else but it. It took the edge off the ache inside him.

"Hey. It's me, Roman. In Tokyo. Well, near it. Airport hotel."

"Oh! Hey. What's up?" Roman could hear the worry in Oscar's voice. "You still coming home, or have they persuaded you to stay?"

Roman chuckled. "Not yet. Nothing could keep me away from good old Tennessee." He rested the side of his head against the bench and closed his eyes. Might as well be honest. "Just wanted to hear a familiar voice."

Oscar paused for a moment and spoke again, his voice gentler. "Yeah, I know that feeling. Or remember it."

Of course he'd get it without him having to say anything more. Roman felt bad that he was rubbing in Oscar's... well, imprisonment, it must feel like. "How's the leg?"

"Eh, so-so. I went for a walk this morning but I can't get as far as I wanted."

Roman grimaced. "Should be further along, shouldn't it?"

"Yeah. I'm seeing the physio again sometime... what day is it anymore? Tomorrow."

"Good. Don't strain it."

Oscar hummed in agreement, then went quiet for a moment before he spoke up. "It's been pretty boring here. J— one of my buddies from the company came by. That was all right."

"Oh yeah? That's nice of him."

"Mm." Oscar didn't sound like he agreed, but Roman didn't want to upset him, so he left it alone. "Then I cleaned the kitchen."

"That bad, huh?"

Oscar laughed under his breath. "Yeah. I'm turning domestic. I'll make a good househusband soon."

Roman caught his breath at that mental image—coming home to a warm kitchen and something freshly made, and

Oscar aglow, talking about what he'd done that day over the dinner table.

"You there?"

"Um. Yeah," Roman answered, pushing himself to his feet. "Just getting out of the hotel gym now. But, uh… I guess when we get back we should talk about… stuff."

Oscar snorted with laughter. "Eloquent. But, fucking *finally*."

"Now who's eloquent?" Roman poked fun back at Oscar, making his slow way down the hall to the elevator. "Yeah. So, I guess I should get to bed."

"That's it? Set up a *we need to talk* and leave me dangling for, what, three days?"

"It's not a bad thing. Is it?" Roman questioned himself. "It's not on my side."

"It's not. I just… you know. We need to know stuff," Oscar said, taking his turn to be vague.

Roman understood why. The thought of *rules* and *labels* and *commitment* was enough to make him itch, even if he yearned for what it meant: stability. Security. A loving embrace at the end of a goddamn long work week.

Maybe that was what he was after, not just putting a ring on it for the sake of it.

"Yeah. Stuff," he agreed quietly. "But for now, uh. Take care. See you real soon."

"See you soon, babe." Roman stared at the phone for a second, but before he could put it to his ear again, Oscar's voice squeaked, he cleared his throat, and he added, "Bye!"

"Bye?" Roman found himself laughing as he pocketed the phone and let himself into his room.

What the hell was going on? After the last few weeks of back-and-forth, most of which he fully recognized was his own fault, at least they were saying *something* about it out loud.

Despite his exhaustion, Roman tossed and turned in bed before his limbs finally grew heavy. A few days' wait had never stretched in front of him so long.

CHAPTER
Thirteen

OSCAR

"Oscar? You're alive!"

As soon as he stepped into the dressing room, his half-naked colleagues swarmed around him, and the speech on his lips died.

He'd spent the morning rehearsing what he was going to say—how disappointed he felt that nobody but Jef had wanted to hang out with him since brunch ages ago, and how he hoped this wasn't going to affect how they treated him when he recovered.

Not *if*, but *when*.

But these were sincere smiles and greetings.

"H-Hi," he answered after a moment, too confused to know what to do as pats to his shoulder and claps on his back welcomed him into the fold. He didn't see Jef immediately. The way the room was constructed, he could have easily been in the showers or water fountain, out of view.

Or putting in extra practice toward his fucking leading role.

"Oscar?" Raj offered a warm smile as he approached, glancing down—unmistakably, at his knee. "Can I have a word?"

It would be mean-spirited to say no, so Oscar nodded despite the most pressing issue on his mind, then caught himself. When had he started caring more about social approval than his career? *Keep it together, Oscar,* he scolded himself.

Raj guided him to a bench in the hallway and sat next to him. "How's recovery going? Three weeks in, right?"

He genuinely cared about Oscar—his career *and* his life—and it put him at ease to be honest. "Slower than I hoped. Stiff and sore a lot. It's getting easier to walk, and I can drive okay now. Maybe by the time you get back from this tour..."

Raj looked skeptical for a moment. "Are you keeping limber? You know eating for recovery isn't the same as eating for performance..."

"I know," Oscar sighed. The protein intake he required was equally high, but he was exercising less. Most dancers were terrified of gaining fat and losing muscle while their exercise regimen was lessened. "I'm eating right. More or less. More junk food," he admitted.

Raj smiled. "I expected that. Have you been thinking about the future, if you're sure you want to come back?"

"I can't go out on *this,*" Oscar immediately defended, his hackles rising. Getting so close to his life's goal that he'd almost *tasted* it, and then unceremoniously dumped? *No.* "No, no, no," he mumbled.

Raj gripped his shoulder. "I understand. But you wouldn't be going out in a blaze of glory. You can stay in the industry—"

"And remember what I lost?" Oscar's voice was sharper, more bitter, than he'd even expected himself. The corners of his eyes pricked with heat but he held it in like any injury, kept his back straight and toes pointed even as he sat.

Raj silently gazed at him, and the compassionate understanding in his expression made Oscar wince.

He knew Raj's own past: lead dancer until he'd gracefully bowed out to join a small company as an artistic director, then larger companies, and finally their very own. But how graceful had that exit been? Rumors swirled, but he'd never asked.

"Sorry," Oscar mumbled, looking down. "I shouldn't take it out on you."

"It's to be expected, darling. I just wanted you to think about the other options. There is no shame in what you've done. You might not have taken leads, but you've gotten good reviews. I've admired your work for years. Your directors have all praised how easy you are to work with. You have real talent, and vision. You understand *why* behind the choreography, you don't just do what you're told."

Oscar glanced at him, startled and pleased and—for the first time in three weeks—glowing with pride.

"If prone to dramatics occasionally," Raj added with a teasing wink.

Oscar was *not* about to admit that he'd spend a day rehearsing a speech about how nobody cared about him anymore. His cheeks flushed and he cleared his throat, folding his arms.

"Go hang out with the other guys." Raj laughed. "They've been missing you."

"Really?"

Raj looked startled. "Yeah. Of course. I think they're going out to eat. You should come." They had a few favorite choice restaurants within walking distance that could cater to their very specific post-workout dietary needs. By now, the chefs probably pulled two dozen plain chicken breasts out of the freezer the moment they walked in.

"I… yeah." Still dazed, Oscar made his way to the dressing room as his friends emerged in twos and threes with cheerful smiles and anecdotes from the last few weeks.

Jef skillfully avoided him by being mysteriously engaged in deep conversation with another dancer as he left the dressing room and headed for those cursed front steps.

Oscar wondered how long it would take before any of them had the courage to ask.

As it turned out, it took until the restaurant. Over lunch, Matt glanced at him. "So, you gonna keep in touch, or do we have to drag you out?"

"I… what?" He'd expected a question about his recovery time, not socializing. "Of course I don't wanna lose touch."

There was a moment of silence at the table, and though they clearly tried not to look his way, several of them glanced at Jef.

"Why'd you think that?" Oscar asked Matt directly. It was kind of cheating; Matt couldn't lie to his face—or anyone's. He was a terrible liar, and everyone knew it.

"Uh." Matt stuttered, then cleared his throat.

The table was entirely silent, and Oscar was aware of Jef's gaze fixed on Matt, too. *He'd better not be getting between Matt and that cute new fiancé of his*, Oscar thought darkly.

Since nobody rescued him, Matt finally said, "Jef said you might want some space now."

Oscar let his eyebrows rise as he turned his head and tilted it slightly, looking down the table at Jef. "Oh? And why would he think to say that?"

"It was in your best interests," Jef defended himself with a touch of unnecessary aggression.

Oscar snorted. "To lose touch with my friends while I'm down and out? My best interests, or yours?"

"I figured the reminder would hurt. Remembering what you lost." His own words thrown back at him—of course Jef had been listening in, the fucking creep. And worst of all, it might be a little true.

Oscar was going to cry if he stayed here a moment later, and he'd be damned if he'd give Jef the satisfaction. Instead, he rose to his feet, hiding the internal wince. He grabbed his wallet and pulled out enough to cover his meal and the drink, then a few ones for the tip, and slammed them on the table.

"Don't you dare speak for me again," he told Jef, his voice quiet but carrying over the rest of the suddenly quiet restaurant.

The graceful exit—storming out, turning his back on the fucking *asshole* trying to add insult and isolation to injury— was undermined slightly since he had to hobble. At least he did that at the fastest pace he could manage, which was speedy indeed.

When the restaurant door finally closed after him, he didn't linger and look back. A smile did finally crack his lips, even if his eyes misted over at the same time. He knew the way back to the studio and his parked car by heart, so he could hang his head and stare at the sidewalk as he tried to compose himself.

Prone to dramatics. Roman is gonna laugh his ass off. When-ever he gets his ass home.

He had to hope his friends—the *real* friends he had there, if any—would straighten Jef out. But Oscar wasn't sticking around to find out. He wasn't sure he could stand one more disappointment.

CHAPTER
Fourteen

ROMAN

THE FRONT DOOR BANGED OPEN, AND A WHIRLWIND OF emotions crossed Oscar's face as he stumbled to a halt in the living room.

"What are you doing here?"

Roman might have laughed, had the flight back gone any better. If Greg hadn't relieved him of duty and sent him for his scheduled sleep rotation, he might have throttled Cory at roughly thirty-three thousand feet.

Instead, Oscar's surprise—even annoyance—at seeing him here in his own home rubbed him the wrong way. All those little daydreams of coming home to a fresh meal were stupid, he knew… they'd never even talked about the idea.

It didn't stop him feeling strangely empty when they were so drastically challenged by reality.

"I'm here because I live here. Are you?"

He regretted it the moment it came out of his mouth, but Oscar just squared his jaw and drew his lithe body up to its full height.

"I don't know. Do I?"

Roman hadn't been ready for that answer. With the wind knocked out of him, it took him a few seconds to regain his composure. "Would you even want to?"

They were approaching each other slowly as if sizing each other up. The closeness, yet shut-off emotion was a stark contrast to the long-distance intimacy they'd shared on the phone just a few days ago.

"Would you want me to?" Oscar countered.

Roman scowled. This was starting to sound like a circular argument, and he hated those. "What do you want, really?"

"I don't know. Not this." Oscar was just arm's-length away now, his gaze intense and unflinching. It felt like a challenge.

Roman reached out slowly to rest his hands on Oscar's waist. When Oscar didn't move away, he pulled him in until they stood toe-to-toe. "Me too."

"Clarity, maybe. What are we doing?" Oscar murmured, his voice still hard-edged but less combative now.

Roman raised his shoulders in a quick shrug. "We weren't supposed to be doing anything."

"And yet," Oscar murmured, his lithe body finally draped against Roman's.

Something inside him uncoiled—something that been waiting for a warm body against his, arms around his shoulders, and finally, lips pressing his.

Roman leaned into the kiss and returned it, slowly but not ignoring the sparks that always ignited.

Kissing was better than talking. It said more, and the memory lasted longer. Even though it had been a constant ache under his skin for the last few days, he hadn't realized how much he needed the physical touch until this moment.

Oscar slid his hands up under Roman's shirt, and Roman knew he was screwed.

"I want you," he murmured against Oscar's lips. He was hardening already, his body responding to Oscar's presence the best way it knew how.

Oscar ground their bodies together, hitching up one leg —the bad one, Roman noted—to carefully lean more weight against Roman. Roman was more than happy to support him, wishing only that there were fewer clothes in the way.

"Take me, then," Oscar murmured.

Roman swept Oscar off his feet in one clean move. He was light enough that it was easy, but solid enough in Roman's arms to knock the wind out of him for a moment.

Or maybe he was just breathless from looking down at the gorgeous man in his arms, meeting his lustful gaze, and trying to choose which of the many daydreams he'd had about the two of them to fulfill tonight.

They were in his bedroom within moments, and Oscar tipped his head to look around the room as Roman brought him to the bed. Roman wondered what he thought of it.

"I could get used to this whole being carried thing." Despite Oscar's light-hearted words, there was another harsh edge to his voice that kept Roman from laughing.

Right. Chalk that up to things not to kill the mood with. Instead, Roman smiled gently. "I could, too."

Oscar snorted at him and pulled him down on top of him roughly. "Don't fuck around with me."

"I'm not!" Roman protested. "I'm going as fast as I can." *We talking about sex, or us?*

"Are you?" Oscar swiftly shrugged his t-shirt off.

Roman gulped. "I am now." He was aching to feel Oscar's

skin against his—even sensually, holding him close, like they had between rounds the first time they'd fucked.

At the same time, he was fully aware, and frustrated at himself for it, that it was his own damn fault they hadn't had time together after their encounters since Oscar moved in.

Normally I need to stop chasing. Maybe with him, I need to stop running.

"Roman," Oscar whispered, pulling Roman's attention back to him as they fought their way out of their clothes. He sounded… needy. That meant Roman wasn't doing his job.

"Sorry," Roman whispered, pressing a kiss to his lips and shoving their discarded clothes out of the way. With their bodies stripped bare, when he let his weight rest on Oscar, it felt like far more than foreplay now.

He ran his hand slowly up Oscar's chest, pausing over his heart to feel the quick thumps.

"Fuck me." Oscar's voice was low but clear. He rolled his head back against the pillow. His hard cock lined up with Roman's as he arched his back and pressed his body up.

Roman couldn't resist dipping his head to kiss the hollow of his throat. He breathed Oscar's scent in—light, fresh water. Aftershave? Had he been dressed up to go somewhere? Whatever he'd been up to, it hadn't gone well judging by his mood.

He pressed kisses along the side of Oscar's neck to his ear, gently flicking his tongue along the lobe. When Oscar was squirming under him, he moved his attention to the sensitive spot behind his ear, running his hand down that narrow chest so he could play with one nipple at the same time.

"Fucking hurry up," Oscar groaned his complaint after a few moments of this. "I said, *fuck me.*"

"Fine," Roman growled under his breath and nipped Oscar's neck, then pulled back to grab lube. *He's really in a mood, isn't he?*

While he did so, Oscar fidgeted under him. He ended up rolling onto his front with his legs pressed together.

"Oh, I see how it is." Roman grinned. "A little doggy-style?"

"Don't know if my knee can support it, but it's worth a shot," Oscar muttered, sounding frustrated.

Roman ran his hand gently down Oscar's back and squeezed that gorgeous ass. "You can lie flat like that. That's fine, too." No way was he setting back Oscar's progress selfishly.

Oscar sighed but said nothing.

He wants to get his mind off it all. Roman could understand that. He could do with distraction from his stupid fucking coworkers and stupid fucking schedule.

Frustration made his movements quick as he slid a slick finger around the tight hole. Oscar pushed into his finger as he pushed inside, his moan quiet and sharp.

"You okay?"

"Of course," Oscar mumbled. "Just get in me."

Roman knew that feeling. It had been a long week—especially without their usual text flirtation. Which was another thought for later—where had that gone? Was that something else he'd stopped? *Shit. I really need to get this dating thing straightened out.*

It felt like too long before he was pressing against Oscar and sinking into him. He shivered with delight at the sensation of being enveloped by tight heat. With his legs pressed together and Roman straddling him, Oscar felt even tighter. "God, I missed you."

"That's your dick talking." Oscar sounded amused, his fingers curled into the comforter underneath.

"It's telling me a lot right now."

"Any pre-dick-tions?" Oscar sounded entirely too satisfied with himself at the pun.

Roman couldn't help it—he laughed richly, then slid his hand up Oscar's back between his shoulder blades as he sank deeper inside, inch by inch. "No puns during sex."

"I suppose I can live with that rule." Oscar turned his head to glance sideways back at Roman, wriggling to try to get a good view of what was going on. "Fuck, yes. It's been too long."

"It's too long?" Roman teased. He kissed the back of Oscar's neck when he pressed his face into the pillow again, slowly pulling back and thrusting again.

"Nnh! No. S'perfect," Oscar grunted.

Oscar was beautiful when his body rippled under Roman's, soft sounds spilling from his lips.

He was never ashamed to ask for what he wanted, and he always gave back as much as he got. It was like he genuinely cared about Roman feeling good, he wasn't just lying there expecting to be given the world. And for some weird reason that he didn't yet understand, Roman wanted to do just that.

Maybe because Roman loved not having to hold back with Oscar. They'd fucked like animals before, and he knew Oscar wasn't breakable. As long as Roman was careful about the injured knee, he could pound Oscar and he would still be begging for more.

Roman set a hard and fast pace, his breathing coming quick and harsh pants across the back of Oscar's neck. He pressed his chest against Oscar's back, letting him feel his weight.

Oscar moaned, reaching behind himself to catch the back of Roman's head and keep him there. "Yes! Like that," he moaned. "Fuck. I missed you."

"Missed you too," Roman managed, his voice a rough growl of desire. There was so much wrapped up in those few little words that he didn't even fully understand yet.

Oscar squirmed under him and gasped with every thrust, his whimpering moans playing counterpoint to Roman's deep noises of approval and pleasure and… well, need.

I do need him. The realization wasn't even a shock, after the week he'd had.

"I'm not gonna last," Oscar laughed under his breath. "Not after all this time."

Roman laughed, too. "We have all night." He rubbed Oscar's hip gently, then redoubled his own pace. He was breathless with the electric charge building under his skin.

His own need was harder to ignore, as much as he tried. Just watching Oscar's back ripple made him hot, let alone hearing the noises he made.

Oscar pushed himself up on his forearms and turned his head for a kiss, so Roman leaned around to meet his lips in an open-mouthed, gasping, desperate kiss.

Then, Roman realized Oscar had worked a hand under himself and was jerking himself off, his whimpers vibrating through Roman's lips as he licked his way into Oscar's mouth.

Then Oscar's eyes slid shut, and he gasped sharply and bucked against him. If he hadn't felt the unbearably good tightness squeezing around him, Oscar's orgasm still would have been unmistakable. His voice caught as he tried to whimper Roman's name, and his hips shuddered forward into his own hand.

"Sexy," Roman gasped. "I'm almost…"

"Keep going. Come for me," Oscar gasped, his cheeks flushed and eyes hazy with pleasure. "Come on, baby. Show me what you've got."

Heat flushed through Roman's cheeks as he thrust a few more times into the quivering heat of his lover's body, and then he finished so hard he could barely breathe. Tingles of pleasure coursed from fingers to toes, up to his scalp, and his world narrowed to Oscar and Oscar alone.

Which was an awfully familiar feeling.

"Oh, fuck," Roman mumbled into Oscar's neck as he collapsed on top of him, sliding his arms under Oscar and around his chest. He held him close as he rolled carefully onto his side and pulled off the condom.

Oscar rested his arms along Roman's, his chest rising and falling in a deep sigh as he let Roman clean up.

"Good?" Roman murmured as his body softened and relaxed.

Oscar chuckled slightly. "Really good. Worth the wait."

"You didn't…" Roman trailed off awkwardly, not sure how to ask. They were just friends, right? He didn't have any right to be jealous. But it wasn't a jealous question, just a… clarity question. "You didn't take off the edge with anyone else?"

"Nope." Oscar said it slowly, popping the "p" sound. That sounded like there was a story there.

"Mm?" Roman murmured.

Oscar shook his head. "Guys are dicks."

Roman's hold tightened as his heart sped up. If anyone had taken advantage of Oscar… "Are you okay?"

"Yeah." Oscar laughed under his breath, then rolled slowly onto his back, shifting so that his head rested on Roman's arm. His eyes were closed, and he was smiling slightly. "I'm good. Better than I thought."

Roman rubbed Oscar's chest gently while he gazed at him. "Good. Me too. Now that I'm home, I mean."

"Sorry I screwed up my days. I was a little stressed and… uh, preparing for dramatics earlier. I thought you were home tomorrow."

Roman chuckled. "Yeah? That explains the weird-ass greeting."

Oscar's cheeks, which had been steadily losing their flush, turned bright red again. "Sorry. That really wasn't cool. I mean, you've been super-generous with your house and stuff…"

"No, no." Roman brushed it off, gently pinching Oscar's chin to turn his head toward him. "I scared you. It's fine."

When Oscar met his gaze, he relaxed. "Okay. But I *am* glad you're home. And that… I'm here. And you're here. You know. Stuff." His gaze flitted away again, like he couldn't quite meet Roman's eyes, and he cleared his throat. "So, cool. Yeah."

Roman let him dodge the bullet, but he was smiling. *This is definitely more than friends.* The thought was ridiculously exciting, and he had to take a few deep breaths to stay cool himself. "Cool. You sleeping here tonight?"

"I'm not hobbling down the hall, so unless you wanna carry me," Oscar rolled his eyes, but the way he said it was tentative, hopeful.

Roman took the chance. "You want to stay?"

After a few long moments, Oscar looked back at him, and he looked adorably flustered. "If you… want me to… yeah?"

Roman winked. "Then stay. Like I said, we have *all* night.

And I don't know about you, but I've got a lot of daydreams to catch up on."

CHAPTER
Fifteen
OSCAR

"You sure you wanna drive me? And wait in the car? It might be a while. It could be boring." Oscar knew damn well he was redirecting his anxiety about the short-notice meeting with Raj.

And, bless him, Roman wasn't calling him out. He just smiled patiently and waved his car keys. "I have a phone. I can keep myself entertained. It's the modern era."

"Fine," Oscar laughed, with a little more amusement than that really warranted. His hands were shaking as he slipped on his shoes and jacket. Truthfully, it was a good thing Roman had offered to drive.

The possibilities were scaring the shit out of him. Especially after the dramatic exit he'd made, and his slow recovery, and Raj's hints yesterday. It was all adding up to form a picture he didn't want to acknowledge.

Deep down, he already knew what Raj was going to tell him, and he wasn't sure he was ready to hear it. In fact, he was certain he *wasn't*.

Wildly, he wondered if he could escape. Disappear, never

show up for his meeting. Change his name? Start a new career?

No. You can't run from this one. You gotta take the punches as well as the flowers. He took as deep a breath as his tight chest would allow. "Let's go."

Roman clapped him on the shoulder, his touch lingering as they stepped through the front door. "Let's blow this pop stand."

The drive was almost silent—Roman gave up on trying to make him talk and just chattered about Tokyo sights, which was a relief. He could tune out and not feel bad, and what he did listen to was actually interesting but didn't require a response. He'd never been so glad that Roman could carry a conversation on one-sided.

Despite the good-luck kiss that lasted a little too long, and included a little more fumbling than was strictly appropriate for parking on the street of downtown Knoxville, he was wound up by the time he got to Raj's office.

The words, expected as they were, stung.

"We can't guarantee your place on the following tour, even if you recover during this show period. I'm not thrilled that Jef's been apparently undermining your social ties—not at all, and I've had a word with him—but from the directors' perspective…"

"No, I get it," Oscar mumbled. Many dancers never reached their skill level again once they let it slip, and this damn knee was still aching too much. Probably because he was too restless to sit still for long. "It's sensible."

"It hurts, I know." Raj reached out over his desk to touch Oscar's hand and get his attention. "But I'm serious—if you stay in the industry, let me help you out. You shouldn't let this be the end, unless you have some other passion or talent you want to explore more."

"I don't have anything in my life except dance," Oscar admitted numbly, almost by routine. Then, he paused. *Except Roman... maybe?* "I mean, and friends." *Shit, I thought of Roman before Falcon. What a shitty best friend I am.* "And, like, uh. Watching TV. Normal stuff." *Unless this means...* "And maybe dating? I can do that now. Date. Without the distance. Unless he has a job with distance." *Oh my god. I like him. Duh.* "I'm not really good at dating."

Raj was laughing quietly as Oscar's panic spiraled. He finally interrupted when he could get a word in edgewise. "Hon. It's all over your face. What's going on?"

"I... I don't know," Oscar admitted. "We haven't really talked. But a friend of a friend is... maybe more than a friend..." He couldn't say more—not in good conscience, without talking to Roman about it. "And he supports me. So that's good, when everything else," he gestured around the office to mean the studio, the company, his life, "is crumbling."

Raj nodded. "Hold onto him," he murmured. "Don't let your bitterness drive him away."

That drew Oscar's eyes to Raj's face, and the emotion he saw there made his throat go tight. "I won't," he promised, and he meant it.

"I'm glad you've got something else—someone else—to focus on while you recover," Raj told him. "And I'm really sorry for having to do this. I won't rub it in any more than I have, but you're a phenomenal dancer. Don't let this keep you down. You apply that grit of yours to anything else and you can do so much."

Except what I want to do more than anything. Oscar

clenched his jaw for a moment to keep the emotion in, then nodded quickly and rose to his feet.

"Don't be a stranger," Raj told him. "Everyone else is going to invite you to *everything* now. And I wouldn't be surprised if Jef gets fewer invites." His kind smile was supposed to make Oscar feel better, but it was a hollow victory when Jef still got what mattered to Oscar.

He barely remembered the walk back out to the car. When Oscar started to slide out of his dazed emotional fog, he was leaning across the center console of the car, his head buried in Roman's chest as Roman held him close.

"I… fuck," Oscar mumbled. "Fuck, it hurts."

"I know," Roman murmured, his hand in Oscar's hair. "Getting fired always sucks. When it's something you loved? I can't imagine."

Oscar nodded. "Exactly. And when *that* asshole got the part instead… oh. Yeah. Don't ask."

"Okay," Roman agreed simply.

Oscar drew a breath of relief. He didn't want to explain the mess with Jef right now. "And now I have no career prospects and I'm getting out of shape and nobody will want me for anything anyway…" Oscar mumbled.

"Look. Hey. It might not count for much, but *I* want you," Roman murmured, slowly and clearly, like he wanted to make sure it sank in.

Was he joking? Fucking with him? Now wasn't the time. Oscar pulled back slightly. "Yeah, yeah," he rolled his eyes.

"No, I mean it." The warmth and affection in Roman's

gaze actually hurt when it so starkly clashed with how Oscar thought of himself right now: a washed-up loser.

Was Roman trying to save him? Or worse yet, was he treating him like all the guys he was with, trying to get too close too fast?

"I don't want your pity," Oscar mumbled, pulling back and buckling up. "I just wanna be ho—" *Home? It's not my home, whatever he says. Don't be presumptuous, idiot.* "I wanna chill out and sit down and just… have a beer. Or six."

"Yep," Roman agreed, giving him an easygoing smile. "That, I can provide."

The drive home was silent this time, but Oscar was too miserable to be uncomfortable. He knew he was indulging the dramatic side of him—some would say wallowing—but the tragedy, the fucking injustice of it…

Roman wasn't telling him everything would be magically better, or that life made obstacles for him to become magically stronger, or any of that bullshit. He was just letting him exist as he was: grieving and bitter and yeah, a little overly dramatic.

Oscar's appreciation for Roman went up several more notches as he let him have these few minutes of silence. He even went ahead to open the car and house doors for him.

When Oscar was finally on the couch, Roman joined him with two open beer cans.

"Thanks."

"Of course." Roman took a deep breath and sat. Before he'd even sipped, his words tumbled out. "I just wanna get out there, good and clear, that our… relationship status, or whatever… whatever we decide to do… it doesn't affect your place here. You can stay here as long as you need to get back on your feet. But, um…"

Oscar waited a few moments while Roman gulped the beer like he was drowning. *What has* him *so rattled?* "But you want rent? That's fair. I've been crashing here for a while."

"What?" Roman yelped. "No, asshole. Not when you just got fired. Jesus."

"Ah. Yeah. Still, it *would* be fair…"

Roman scoffed. "Shut up."

"Fine," Oscar laughed sheepishly and ducked his head. He couldn't think what else it was, unless… no way. He wasn't going to get his hopes up.

"*But*," Roman continued pointedly, rolling his eyes at Oscar until Oscar laughed, "I, uh. About us. I mean." He gulped again and put the can on the coffee table, folding his hands. "But I don't know if I can keep fucking you without being allowed to love you, too."

A few seconds slipped by before Oscar could get his brain working enough to understand. Even then, he wasn't sure he'd heard right. "You what?"

"I… need some kind of…" Roman made vaguely box-shaped movements with his hands. "Idea. What we're doing. What you'd let me do. I mean, I don't want to rush you, but things are so… I didn't think you'd even want me. I've been so fucking hot and cold, I know. And I'm sorry about that. But it's hard not to fall for you, and… oh god, I'll shut up now."

The first word that came to Oscar's mind made him grin slowly. "Slick."

"Shut *up*," Roman groaned.

Oscar couldn't help but sympathize. The poor guy had just put his heart on the line. "Sorry. You're adorable when you do that. I like you too."

"What?" Roman looked just as surprised. "But you don't... date..."

"Neither do you." Oscar raised an eyebrow. "Or you scare them off by committing too fast, you said once."

"Was this too fast? Jesus. Sorry. I'll, like, let you have your time. Or whatever you need."

"No, man." Roman looked like he was about to hyperventilate, and Oscar felt about the same way himself. "It's just... a big deal for us both. I need to think about this before I promise you anything, you know? Don't want to make promises I can't keep," Oscar told him softly, taking his hand and squeezing. "We'll pick this up in a bit, okay?"

"Cool. Yep. Good." Roman looked relieved as Oscar stood up. He picked up the TV remote upside-down and tried to mash the DVD eject button instead of turning it on. The DVD player opened and he mumbled a curse, mashing the button again.

Roman was even more flustered than him. Oscar couldn't stop himself grinning, even as he fled to the comfort of his room and closed the door gently, yet firmly.

Shit. It was all out there now.

He paced back and forth for a few minutes, even limping as he was, trying to let his brain turn over the implications of what lay beyond that door: Roman.

He wanted him. He liked him. *Romantically.* That was weird and new. But weird and new didn't mean *bad.* Falcon sure seemed happy enough with his relationship these days.

Things like distance might be hard to work out, but they'd managed so far. If they started actually talking about their feelings, they probably could make it work, right?

But did Roman *really* like him? Or was he just trying to

settle for someone nearby again? From what Falcon had let on, and what Roman had let slip, that was Roman's pattern.

This wasn't something he could call Falcon about. Even if it weren't for the fact that he was sleeping with his best friend's boyfriend's best friend, which was a convoluted sentence, Falcon couldn't tell him more about Roman than he already knew. His heart had to decide what to do, and he wasn't good at listening to it.

Oscar had to stop irritating his knee, though. He crashed on the bed and closed his eyes, waiting to see where his mind went.

Roman was there for me today. Every time he's home, he is. Hell, he's there by text most of the rest of the time. He doesn't ask questions, he doesn't need me to be someone else...

"Shit." Oscar opened his eyes and stared at the ceiling as the inescapable truth sank in.

Under his breath, so softly he could barely hear it himself, he whispered, "I want you, too." It sounded right. It *was* right. It was way too late to worry about falling for Roman when he'd already gone and done that.

Roman was clearly sincere. He'd done more for Oscar than he'd ever needed to, and out in the living room when he'd talked about love, he'd looked scared out of his mind. Which was about the same as Oscar felt about the possibility.

But, like it or not, *something* was developing between them, and the thought of pulling away now hurt too much to even consider.

There was only one possible answer.

CHAPTER
Sixteen

ROMAN

"You're telling me you want out? Already?" Harold sounded astonished.

Roman couldn't blame him. He'd probably react the same way, in Harold's shoes. "I know, I know. I got lucky even getting that route. But the long-hauls are... I don't know, man. They're messing with things."

As always, Harold cut to the chase. "*Things*. I hate that word, kid. Your sleep schedule, or your sleep *with* schedule?"

"Uh. A bit of both." Roman glanced toward the guest room door again, then sighed and paced the living room into the kitchen, leaning on the island. Anything to stop himself getting neck strain staring at the door.

Oscar had to think about it. Roman had to give him space, especially with all the other big life events going on for him. He wasn't going to use that place of insecurity to pressure him.

Even if he did desperately want answers on how much Oscar was prepared to give him.

"So you want, what, back to short-hauls? Hopping around America all day long?"

"Yeah, if I can get switched back to short-hauls… I mean, I was talking to people who said it should be easy. We both know how much demand there is on the long-haul routes." Roman had had to wait over a year to get his position on the roster.

"Well, I won't say you're crazy, but it all depends what you've got lined up, kid. If it's what you want, they can't stop you. You're good enough you can walk to another airline— though you won't find another one based outta Knoxville. Nashville, you've got a swinging chance."

"I don't know. It can't hurt to ask, right?"

"Right."

"Thanks, Harold. I'd better let you get back to watercolor painting, or whatever it is you do these days," Roman teased.

"Painting my new girlfriend, more like."

"Oh, God." Roman didn't want that mental image, but now he had it. "Thanks, man."

"Anytime."

When he turned around, he nearly jumped out of his skin. Oscar was silently leaning in the doorway, having moved with surprising speed. How long had he been there? "Jesus, man. Make a guy have a heart attack."

Oscar half-smiled, but he was already clearly fixated on something. His gaze never left Roman's face, the adorable wrinkle between his brows creasing like it did when he was deep in thought. Or about to be dramatic. Roman knew which one he was hoping for. "Switching to short-haul routes?"

Roman swallowed hard, then nodded at the couch. "We should talk?" he offered.

"Yeah, I think so." Oscar refused Roman's offer of an arm and limped heavily over to the couch, settling himself carefully. It was always awkward and painful to watch the last few seconds of him trying to sit without moving one leg too much.

Roman settled next to him, keeping a safe "friend" distance between them. "So you had a chance to think about things?"

Oscar's mouth twisted into a quick smile. "Yeah. And then I heard *that*. What the fuck's that about?"

"Me... switching routes?"

"Yeah. You told me long-hauls were your dream." Oscar watched him intently, his expression hard to read.

Roman suddenly felt like he was being interrogated, and he folded his hands carefully. "Um. It's not the easiest schedule to manage sometimes. And if you and me... I mean, I'm not assuming anything... but it's hard to spend days apart, or even a week sometimes. If I fly short-hauls, I'm home nearly every evening."

"Don't you fucking dare give up your dreams so easily. Especially not if it's for *me*." Oscar folded his arms.

Roman let out his breath slowly. It was suddenly clear where this was coming from. He should probably tread lightly. He couldn't think of any way to bring it up delicately, though, so he plunged in. "Do you feel like you have?"

Oscar flinched, then nodded, his expression guarded. "You know that."

"Today of all days, yeah. But it's not about that at all," Roman told him firmly, sliding closer to him on the couch to touch his shoulder. "I'm sorry it's been such a shitty day. I shouldn't have brought *us* up now."

"No," Oscar mumbled, his face finally losing the guarded

quality as he relaxed into the touch. He scooted slightly closer and Roman took that as his cue to wrap his arm around Oscar's shoulders, pulling him in. "It's fine," Oscar insisted, even as his voice went thick.

Roman rubbed his back again, pressing his nose into his hair. *I really will have to figure out what his shampoo is that smells so great. Not the right moment, though, dude.* "Still. I'm sorry about all of it. It sucks, man."

"It does," Oscar agreed, clearing his throat a few times. He tried pulling away. "Sorry. I don't wanna get all…"

"Baby," Roman murmured, the name slipping out before he could even think about it. "It's okay. You need someone to listen and be here. If that's all you want, that's okay."

Oscar pulled away and shook his head, his lips set in that stubborn line that meant he knew he was fighting a losing battle but was damn well going to try anyway. He was so easy to read, it was utterly charming.

"What's wrong with that?"

"I don't want to use you."

Roman paused and stared at Oscar, his arm still loosely around his shoulders. "What?"

"While I'm this…" Oscar gestured around, searching for words, his gaze sliding from Roman's face to the floor. "This much of a mess."

Roman felt like he was missing half the conversation. "But that's when I *want* to be here for you."

"But that's just using you for… feeling better, and…" Oscar trailed off. He rubbed his face and sighed, then slid his hand into Roman's, linking their fingers. He reached up with his left hand to touch the one on his shoulder. "I'm not great at this relationship stuff. Obviously. My parents splitting and all, and I never had time for one…"

Roman squeezed Oscar's hand and pulled him against him again. "It's fine, hon. But that's not how relationships work. You love someone at their lowest just as fiercely, if not more." He straightened up, his belly burning with the truth he was speaking. "You stand up for them when everyone else is being a dick. You give them a shoulder to cry on. You're there when they come home, you know? You're there, safe and warm and cozy, for them. Love is a haven."

Oscar was watching him, his expression soft and… hopeful? "That all… I mean, that all sounds too good to be true."

"How do you mean? Just because you haven't had it before?" Roman asked, then interjected, "I'm assuming here."

"I haven't. I can't figure out why…" Oscar's voice tightened and cracked, but though Roman tried to brush it off, he wouldn't let it go. "Why you'd want me like this."

"I want you to let me take care of you when you need it," Roman murmured. "And it's not one-sided. I promise I have my bad days, too. But you can't decide *for* me what I can handle."

Oscar's lips parted slightly as he stared at Roman, like he hadn't considered it.

"And," Roman added ruefully, "I know that yeah, I was kind of doing that for you. By running away from talking about all of this." He squirmed slightly, the guilt pooling in his stomach. "I'm trying to do better now."

"Talk?" Oscar scoffed. "I don't like talking it out. Not when we could be doing much better things with our mouths. That's the kind of relationship I like." His eyes glinted in a challenge.

Roman grinned back at him. "That could be arranged."

"Yeah? Then…" Oscar raised his shoulders in a slight shrug. "We'll take it slow. Try it out." Despite his attempt to be subtle, Roman's delight must have been obvious. Oscar laughed and added, "Well, if I'd known that was all it took to make you grin like a loon. Happy?"

Roman's cheeks burned. "Uh. Yeah. I'm happy. I like this. This dating thing. I think." *Dating. Saying it out loud is weird. Wow.*

"Dating," Oscar repeated, rolling it off his tongue. Then he turned toward Roman on the couch, his eyes glinting. "That means more sex? And sleeping together? For convenient middle-of-the-night sex?"

"That definitely means more sex, if you want more sex," Roman laughed. "If *I'd* known that was all it took to get *you* to say yes…"

"I want a lot of sex, if you hadn't already noticed." Oscar laughed. "Does that make me sound shallow?"

Roman shook his head and growled, "If you are, so am I." He nipped Oscar's ear and wriggled his fingers out from Oscar's to squeeze his thigh.

"We speak the same language," Oscar breathed, his eyes glinting with amusement. "We can make this work."

That sounded promising. Roman tried not to get his hopes up, but it was impossible after this conversation. Taking it slow with anyone was the ultimate challenge, but if that was what it took to make Oscar see he really did want him, he had no choice.

He swooped in to kiss Oscar hard, wrapping his arms around his shoulders and sliding his hands along Oscar's back.

Oscar moaned and went limp in his arms the moment Roman bit his lower lip. He was already working his hands under Roman's shirt, running his nails up his back.

"Lie back," Roman told Oscar, grinning as he slid off the

couch onto his knees. He carefully slid his hand under Oscar's bad leg, glancing up at him to make sure he was fine as he lifted, helping him lie flat on the couch.

"I can do that myself," Oscar mumbled, but half-heartedly. His eyes were wide with desire.

"But then I can do this," Roman murmured, running his hands slowly up Oscar's inner thighs as he watched his face.

"Fuck," Oscar hissed, spreading his legs as one foot slipped off the couch. "Get up here."

"I love it when you try to get bossy," Roman teased. He stayed on his knees next to the couch, leaning down to bite Oscar's lip slowly and deliberately. He whispered, "I have other ideas."

He rubbed the hard shaft with his palm as he spoke, letting his thumb press around the ridge of the head of Oscar's cock. His other hand popped open the button on Oscar's jeans.

"D-Do you?" Oscar's voice was weak. He gripped Roman's shoulder so hard his nails dug in again. "Hurry up with them, 'cause I'm gonna embarrass myself soon."

Roman smirked and ducked his head to kiss Oscar again, then grabbed his shirt and pulled it off. As much as Oscar worried about his body, his desirability at work and in love, Roman found him fucking hot.

Maybe more so now that he'd lost the edge of almost inhuman perfection. Rippling abs, thighs of steel, and biceps that could stifle a stray toddler looked wrong when he was actually trying to picture himself *with* Oscar... like something statuesque. Now, Oscar looked better: he had that healthy glow.

He realized he was staring at Oscar's body and, with difficulty, pulled his gaze up to his face again.

"Inspecting the goods?" Oscar smirked at him.

"You bet." Roman took Oscar's hand and guided it to his hard shaft, letting him go as Oscar rubbed lightly. That sent prickling, tingling pleasure through his body, his sight hazy for a moment. "Now do you believe I want you just like you are? No matter what?"

Oscar swallowed hard. "I don't know why, but I'm starting to believe it." His voice wavered.

"Let me show you." Roman pinched Oscar's zipper between two fingers and dragged it down, then helped him shift so his jeans pulled tight around his thighs, leaving his hard cock poking up into the air. He pointedly licked his lips.

Oscar gasped. "Oh, fuck! Yes!" he mumbled, his thighs twitching in anticipation. He squeezed Roman's shaft through his jeans and rubbed a little harder.

Spurred on, Roman kissed the outside of Oscar's thigh, then licked from the base to tip a few times, enjoying every vocal reaction he wrung out of Oscar.

"Let me," Roman murmured, pushing Oscar's hand away from himself. He could take care of that later. "Just relax."

"Are you sure?" Oscar murmured, his eyes flickering open to stare at Roman.

"Relax, baby." Roman ran his hand up Oscar's chest to play with a nipple. "This is all for you." Oscar's full-body twitch and moan was delightful to the ear, and Roman carefully ran his thumb around the nub a few more times before he flicked it again.

"Fuck," Oscar moaned, trying to grind against Roman's lips. "Suck me. Please."

Roman gently pinched the sensitive skin along Oscar's shaft between his lips while being careful not to nip. When he reached the head again, he swirled his tongue around it and slowly sucked the shaft into his mouth.

The series of small noises that tumbled from Oscar's lips were deliciously addictive. Roman shivered and sucked harder as he ran his fingers around Oscar's nipples in gentle, teasing circles.

"*Fuck*," Oscar repeated himself, his hips shivering, probably with the effort not to thrust up. Roman helped him out by sliding his other hand down to hold his hip to the sofa, slowly sliding the shaft further into his mouth.

When Oscar bumped the back of his throat, Roman moaned gently and pulled his head back up, setting an excruciatingly slow pace to tease Oscar for as long as he could. Plus, there was a selfish reason. He tasted divine and the heavy, silken weight of him on Roman's tongue felt right. Roman wanted this to last forever.

Oscar's breath came in quick hisses and pants. "You feel amazing," he groaned, his skin shivering and rippling. It felt intoxicating to be in charge, making Roman lose his mind with pleasure. He was throbbing with pleasure, his pants way too tight.

Roman spared himself a hand to free and stroke himself a few times to try to calm down, then returned his finger to tweaking Oscar's nipple. He sucked his cheeks in, lapping the sensitive frenulum.

God, his dick is gorgeous. If Roman's mouth weren't so full, he'd tell him as much. He settled for glancing up toward Oscar's face as he kissed the shaft again, then gazing at the pink, stiff skin under his lips with an appreciative look.

Oscar turned red but smiled, too, looking suddenly shy as he closed his eyes. "You're too good. I'm so close…"

Roman didn't answer, just kept bobbing his head. He

freed Oscar's hips from his tight grip, instead gently squeezing his balls and running his hand along his thigh. Every single sensation he could think of giving Oscar at once, he did.

The last traces of Oscar's self-restraint came undone as his lover grabbed the back of his head and moaned. "I'm so… fuck… can I?"

Roman answered in a moan around Oscar's shaft and freed up his hand to press over Oscar's, making it clear he could thrust up as he needed.

"Yes! Oh my God, Roman. You're so hot. Needed this so much," Oscar panted, his voice faint. "Needed you. F-Fuck… *yes!*"

Roman swallowed as warm, thick passion coated his tongue, making sure Oscar had a good view. Oscar actually tasted *good*, too. When Oscar collapsed on the sofa, Roman licked the shaft a few more times and stroked gently, then leaned against the sofa and grinned up at him. "So?"

Oscar's eyes were half-closed, his cheeks flushed red. "I… my… that… yeah." He tangled his hand more gently in Roman's hair this time, pulling him towards him. "Kiss me?"

How could Roman resist that soft plea? He shifted on hands and knees until he could lean in and kiss Oscar.

"Come on. Your turn," Oscar encouraged. When Roman tried to protest, he grinned. "You turning down a blank canvas?"

Even thinking of Harold's words half an hour ago couldn't dampen Roman's spirits at the invitation. His heart pounded as he pushed himself to his feet slowly. "Really?"

Oscar's eyes were already hungrily fixed on his cock. "Pleease. I wanna feel that hot load you've got waiting for me. Let me taste it. Come on," he wheedled.

Roman's cock twitched as the muscles in his body went tight, the blood rushing south. *Oh, fuck. He's got a dirty mouth.* "I... *fuck*. Oscar."

"You wanna be in charge? We're dating now, huh? Mark me. Show me I'm yours." Oscar wasn't stopping, his eyes glinting with mischievous pleasure. "That turns you on, huh?"

"Fucking right it does." Roman didn't waste a moment bracing himself on the back of the couch, his hand tight around his shaft. He stroked hard and fast, unable to tear his gaze away from that beautiful face he'd utterly fallen for without quite realizing it.

But those morose few weeks of back-and-forth were over. Oscar was here, with him, giving him a chance. Not just at sex, but at a life together.

He groaned and gasped as he came, and Oscar pushed himself up on his elbows to make sure he coated his chest, chin, tongue...

"Yes!" Roman whimpered and just about lost his balance as Oscar deftly closed his lips around the head of his cock and licked away the last few drops, then flopped back on the couch again, covered in Roman's mess.

The sight blew most of the circuits in his brain. He simultaneously blushed and stared, his nails still digging into the couch as he tried to catch his breath. "Oh my *God*. You're so fucking good."

Oscar smirked. "Weren't expecting my filthy mouth?" He wiped a finger along his jaw pointedly and sucked it clean.

It was pretty fucking hard to embarrass Roman, but he knew he was blushing. "I should've known by now." When his knees were solid again, he grabbed tissues and cupped Oscar's cheek, wiping him clean.

Oscar lay still and let him clean up, his smile warm and affectionate. It made Roman just about shake with nerves.

This was the part he wasn't sure about. They'd managed that one night to sleep together, but it wasn't bedtime. He couldn't really tell him he loved him—it felt too soon, too likely to scare him off—but if anything, he was dead certain now. If this wasn't mature, whole-hearted love, the seed was there with Oscar, where he'd only felt desperately hopeful before now.

Seed. So to speak. Roman was still blushing, laughing under his breath as he thought that.

"What?" Oscar murmured, smiling.

"Nothing," Roman mumbled, awkwardly clearing his throat.

Oscar scooted backward and sat up, then turned to lower his feet to the floor carefully. "Come here," he murmured. "If we're dating, I'm going to be obnoxiously snuggly."

Roman beamed as he sat, wrapping his arm around Oscar again and leaning back. "Cool. You do you, and I'll like it."

"I think I could live with that," Oscar murmured. He closed his eyes and pressed his cheek against Roman's shoulder.

Roman settled back to enjoy the thrum of pleasure still vibrating through his body. "I think so, too."

Seventeen

OSCAR

"IS THIS THE PLACE?"

Roman was a little too tall and broad for Oscar's subcompact car. He leaned down to get a better look out the window, then checked his phone. "I think so." He cast one more reproachful look at Oscar.

They'd spent half the drive debating the merits of Oscar strengthening (or, as one side of the argument would have it, *damaging*) his kneecap muscles by driving unnecessarily. Oscar wasn't about to get into it again. He just smiled and shut off the car. "Good luck to us."

"Hold on." Roman had been fidgety all morning, and Oscar suspected he knew why. "Um... about *us*..."

"Are we going to tell them?" Oscar guessed at his question.

"Yeah. Are we?"

Roman frowned and looked away, and Oscar followed his gaze, inspecting Falcon and Blane's new house. It was a little shabby, but easily updated with some elbow grease and artistic talent, which between them, they had in spades.

"I don't know," Oscar admitted, nudging Roman to get him to look over. "I kind of want to keep it… just us for now."

Roman looked relieved. His breath rushed out in a sigh. "Yes. I mean, it's so new…"

"And they don't think we can do it."

"Yeah. I don't want the—"

"—scrutiny?"

"Exactly."

They smiled at each other.

"Fuck," Roman muttered. "We're finishing each other's sentences already. How easy is it gonna be to hide?"

Oscar laughed. "I'm sure we can manage. Don't shove your tongue down my throat and we'll be golden."

Roman looked wounded. "I don't kiss like that. Do I? You've never said."

"No," Oscar assured him and laughed again. "You're an excellent kisser. But you're losing the point. Stay with me, man."

"I can follow multiple conversations," Roman said, drawing himself up in what was probably supposed to be dignified mock offense.

"Are you going to brag it's a pilot thing?"

"It's part of the—what? No," Roman scoffed hastily, his cheeks flushing. "I mean, it's just a thing."

"Uh huh. Those four bars, on the shoulder of a hot young thing like you? You can't tell me you don't use them," Oscar smirked.

"It worked on you." Roman winked. "*Now* who's losing the point?"

Oscar swatted him. "Oh, God. We're never going to fake it, are we?"

Roman laughed with him. "Just don't admit to anything. It's our business what we do."

"Is it too weird? Like… keeping a secret?" Oscar asked. "I mean, you guys are all like brothers."

"No," Roman said quickly. "No, it's fine. It's not hurting anyone. It just feels like… it's something just for *us* while we figure it out. I mean, unless you want to jump to labels and automatic plus-ones…"

Oscar made a face. "Good point," he admitted. "I have no idea how all that stuff works." In reality, he'd dated a few guys, but he'd never lived with the guy while in the early stages of deciding if it even *would* be a relationship. This was a whole new ballgame. He didn't want anyone else screwing with it yet, even with the best of intentions. "Something to guard for a little while, as it grows."

"So I'm not the only romantic in this car," Roman grinned. The way he watched Oscar made him feel like his blasé attitude wasn't fooling anyone, and that more than even his words made Oscar blush.

"Shut up. Let's get inside before they think we're swapping head in the car."

Roman's brows rose in a way that made Oscar almost, but *not at all*, regret making the joke. "I'll keep *that* in mind," he promised in a low tone.

"Anyway!" Oscar found himself almost falling out of the car in an attempt to get out before he had to find something to hold in front of himself. *That wouldn't be obvious at all.*

He leaned heavily on the car, and Roman came around. "Let me help you, at least."

Oscar eyed him.

"No funny business… in front of them, anyway," Roman

winked. "But for real. If we're standing eight feet apart at all times, it'll be obvious, too. Just relax. Be natural."

"I trained for a stage. I know how to act natural," Oscar retorted.

Roman grinned wickedly, and Oscar knew what was coming before he even said it. "Oh, now who's bragging?"

"We sound like an old married couple already," Oscar grumbled, and he didn't miss the flash of hope that crossed Roman's face. Nor did he mind the idea, really, when he thought about it.

Fuck. We're so screwed.

It took them a minute to get up the driveway, Oscar's arm around Roman's shoulder so he could rest as little weight as possible on his bad knee.

They were barely at the door before Falcon yanked it open. "You made it! We don't have a lot of furniture yet, but the delivery guys just left, and oh my God, I haven't seen you in *weeks*!" He grabbed Oscar for a tight, long hug, and then gave Roman a quick hug, too. "Oh my God, your knee. Sit down. Come in."

Oscar laughed. "It's better than it looks," he promised. "Just taking precautions."

"You said the physio said you're healing slower than you thought?" Falcon closed the door after them and led them through to a den with just a small sofa and coffee table.

Oscar was very conscious of his arm around Roman's shoulder and Roman's steadying hand, but he tried to play it cool. "Yeah. Wow, this place is great," he murmured as he sank onto the couch and found a comfortable angle to prop his knee up.

The vaulted ceilings gave the house an airy feel, and the hardwood floors were gorgeous. He could immediately see

Falcon's taste in the place. Much like that cute little loft, but on a bigger scale. There was more room for two here. *Or more.*

His best friend beamed. "Thanks!" He was hovering, predictably enough. "Do you need anything? Water? Juice? Beer?"

Before Oscar could tell Falcon that he wasn't actually unable to move or fetch anything, Blane interrupted. "Hey, guys!" Roman's best friend made straight for Roman for a manly, back-slapping hug. "What do you think?"

"It's awesome," Roman agreed, gesturing around. "Really light and spacious. A little dated, but…"

"Yeah, that's what I was talking about," Blane enthused, coming to perch on the arm of the sofa and hug him around the shoulders. "It'll be a great DIY project. We're starting with painting and wallpaper, if Falcon doesn't kill me for my taste in decorations."

"You keep refusing to tell me which option you prefer," Falcon accused him, laughing as he joined Blane and pecked his cheek. "You're telling me you *do* have preferences?"

"Nope. Whatever you want, honey."

It sounded so dutiful—yet playful—that Oscar laughed. "Jesus, you two are sickeningly adorable." Something teasing flashed through Falcon's expression as he glanced between Oscar and Roman, who had sat down right next to him. Before he could say anything, Oscar continued, "So, is this the living room?"

"Actually, no," Falcon happily took up the thread of conversation, chattering for a few minutes about their plans: turn this room into an art studio, stick with the one living room near the back of the house, redo the kitchen cabinets…

Blane finally interrupted, "How's the knee? Dude, that brace looks rough."

"Ugh." Oscar pulled a face. He'd resorted to wearing long shirts and sweaters with leggings, so he could pull the brace on over the leggings and not chafe the skin around his kneecap. Only having a couple pairs of jeans that would fit over it was getting old. "I'll be glad to get it off. Roman's been trying to get me to sit still…"

Falcon snorted. "Good luck with *that*," he told Roman.

"I know," Roman laughed while Oscar glared at them both. "He even drove here."

"*Oscar*," Falcon exclaimed.

"Oh god. I'm going to be suffocated by bubble wrap if they have their way," Oscar groaned. "Save me," he pled of Blane.

Blane held up his hands. "Hey. I know whose bed I have to share tonight." He mimed zipping his lips.

"Fair enough," Oscar laughed. But that led them right back to the same subject.

"Speaking of which—"

Oscar was blushing. He knew it. He couldn't stop it, and if he feigned a sudden allergy to the sunlight pouring through the front window, it would make it even more obvious. He just tried to say nothing and give nothing away with his expression.

To his relief, Falcon continued as if he hadn't noticed. "That house must be getting cramped for you two. And I'm home here most of the time, now that I've turned in the keys for the old loft. We have spare rooms. Getting a mattress is easy."

"No, no," Roman waved off the offer. "Unless, uh, Oscar wants a break."

"No," Oscar quickly chimed in. "Thanks, man, but you've got enough to sort out. And I don't feel like dying of paint fumes. I've done that enough in your loft," he teased.

Falcon laughed sheepishly. "Yeah. I think I've killed half my sense of smell by now. But are you sure? Things have to be…" he paused, fishing for words while Oscar tried not to roll his eyes. "Unstable."

"With me being unemployed now?" Oscar said dryly. "I noticed. But nah."

"Nobody ever uses my guest room these days, now that Nico and Deen live together here," Roman added with a nod. "It's good to have company, actually."

Unexpectedly, Blane smiled. "Good. I was getting worried about that bachelor shtick."

"Oh, fuck off," Roman told him. They playfully tussled for a moment across Oscar, who leaned back and well out of the way.

"Boys," Falcon rolled his eyes at Oscar, who just laughed.

Watching the guys interact was always sweet. They had that rare kind of friendship that made it clear why they considered each other brothers every time they were together.

Just like his own friendship with Falcon. But now that Blane and Falcon had a life together, he couldn't encroach on that.

Hell, he was encroaching enough on Roman, crashing at his home with no end date in sight and no job prospects. Everyone else around him—not just these three, but the rest of the brothers, and his former coworkers—had a rich life. Work, and careers, and life goals. The kind of stuff that he'd blinked and lost.

No. No feeling sorry for myself. I have to get my shit together.

He sat back as everyone else made pointed conversation about neutral subjects, even though Falcon kept throwing him careful looks, as if to make sure he wasn't secretly depressed as fuck.

Even if he was, there was no point in sitting around and feeling sorry for himself while everyone tiptoed around the subject so as not to upset him. That only made him feel worse.

If dancing wasn't an option, Oscar had to figure out if he could coach it somehow, or get into choreography, or... any of the myriad options that felt inferior right now, but were *something* better than sitting around.

If he let this knee dictate what he was going to do, he was going to go crazy before it was ever healed. And Oscar had trained far too much under far too ruthless teachers to be the kind of guy who lay around waiting for life to happen.

It was time to take charge.

CHAPTER
Eighteen
ROMAN

"Oscar? Are you there?"

Roman paused and cocked his head to listen, then frowned as only silence greeted him after a few seconds. He wandered into the living room and leaned around the couch enough to see the open door of Oscar's room. He wasn't in there, then.

"Or have you left the house without telling me? Again."

He added the last word in a mutter, just in case he *was* there, but still no answer. Roman sighed and wandered the house once more to make sure Oscar hadn't fainted somewhere, then flopped on the couch.

He grabbed the remote and put it aside again. The only thing on would be bad daytime TV, and that never improved his mood. Instead, he folded his arms and crossed an ankle over his knee.

This is better than watching him limp around, I guess. Though actually, it isn't, because now I'm imagining it probably worse than it is.

"Just because I would have lectured you about driving

with a bad knee like a dumbass doesn't mean you shouldn't tell me you're about to go drive with a bad knee," he muttered under his breath, finally unable to resist. "Okay. Great. Now you're talking to yourself. Good job, man."

Christmas was coming up. Maybe Oscar was out shopping. Speaking of which, Roman should really think about buying things for at least his family, the significant brothers, and Oscar. Plus his coworkers. And now his brothers' new boyfriends… the gift list grew longer every year.

Roman stood up and paced around the house once more. He needed to get out and do something—find another hobby, maybe.

Just as he had the thought, his phone rang. He let out a breath, grateful for the interruption. Then, he paused. The only people who called landlines anymore were bosses.

Well, he *was* cleared to work. No alcohol in the last few days. He never made it a habit to drink every evening like certain pilots who didn't want to find themselves called in at short notice.

"Not doing anything else," he muttered to himself and grabbed the phone. "Hello?"

Someone had gone and caught some terrible tropical fever, which meant he was still bound for Singapore but leaving a day early—tonight.

Only when he was packing his suitcase did Roman realize it had never occurred to him to say no. He'd never had a reason to turn down overtime before. A couple nights in a hotel, familiar bars, new boys, and a few hours' paid work in the air each way. Easy choice.

He blew out a quick sigh. Oscar had been in and out of the house for the last couple days, and he hadn't said a word about what he was up to. Socializing or physio or something,

Roman assumed. He wasn't going to be nosy. Oscar would say when he was ready.

Except now he was about to hop on a flight and leave the guy he was dating without a word. "Crap." He grabbed his phone and dialed Oscar's number.

Straight to voicemail.

Roman tried again, with the same result, and then blew out a sigh and left his suitcase by the front door. As he shrugged on his jacket, he hurried to the kitchen counter and grabbed scrap paper to scrawl a quick note.

Hey— here, he hesitated, deciding whether to use a pet name or not. If he brought a friend home or something, it would be a dead giveaway. He used Oscar's name instead, and shook his head at how much time he'd wasted deciding on that.

Work called me in early. I'm flying to Singapore tonight instead of tomorrow night. I tried calling but didn't get through. Hope you're OK, text me when you can. I'll receive them when I land. Photos to come...

XOX Roman

That wasn't terribly subtle, but he grinned to himself. Assuming Oscar was fine—and Roman assured himself again that he probably *was*, he was just busy with something—he ought to pick up the hint.

It wasn't quite a goodbye blowjob, but it would do.

"Welcome to the B-crew. Sorry our Petey got sick and hauled you in early. Big plans in Singapore?" Ken winked cheerily as they breezed through security and headed to the gate.

Roman zipped up his roller bag and followed. "Not yet."

He was the youngest captain in the fleet; most of his first officers were his own age, so they liked to swap stories while the older captains who'd settled into married life enjoyed living vicariously through them. Or, more often, joined in.

Pilots led an unusual lifestyle, especially as viewed from the outside world. Roman tried not to spill too many details to his family at holiday parties. He wasn't sure it would make everyone feel safer in the skies to know what aerospace employees got up to in their downtime.

Holidays. Crap. He and Oscar had to figure things out before the holiday season. If he was going to visit his parents this year, he didn't want to subject a new boyfriend to their attention. And Oscar's parents... that had to be a delicate situation.

"That doesn't sound like you." Ken paused and glanced at him. "Everything all right?"

"Oh, fine. Yeah. Just a quiet weekend away for me," Roman told him with a forced smile. *A quiet weekend alone in a hotel room.* He'd gotten used to these last few nights going to sleep with Oscar in his arms, or at least touching his arm or chest.

He missed that touch already, and the sound of Oscar's breathing growing deep and steady as he drifted to sleep after a blissful, sex-filled evening, and the smell of Oscar's shampoo on his pillow.

He missed Oscar, and he hadn't even taken off yet.

Crap. I have to do something about this.

"No pretty dates waiting for you?" Ken prompted, his brow furrowing. "You know I don't mind hearing about it."

That drew Roman's attention. "Huh? Yeah, of course. Why?"

Ken looked guilty for a moment, then cleared his throat. "I was on the deck with Cory…" He trailed off meaningfully.

"Oh, for fuck's sake," Roman muttered under his breath. "Yeah, I know he's running his mouth about me. He didn't start rumors or any crap like that, did he?"

"No," Ken quickly reassured him. "Nah, nothing like that. Just dropping hints about how *you guys* have wilder party weekends than the rest of us. That kind of stuff. I told him to knock it off and he seemed pretty surprised."

Roman grimaced. "Thanks," he muttered, resenting that Ken had even had to step in on his behalf.

"Keep an eye on it, huh?" Ken advised him with a clap to his shoulder. "Talk to someone at HR if he gets weird about it."

He's way past weird about it. But Roman wasn't going to give in to a little hazing and make the situation worse by talking to the bosses. He'd made it through flight school, after all. He just nodded once, shortly.

"Anyway, you just proved him wrong," Ken grinned, obviously trying to lighten the mood. "A whole weekend in Singapore and no boys lined up… ohhh." He glanced over. "Got another boyfriend?"

"Yeah, another boyfriend," Roman echoed, half-paying attention. It was true—he'd had a string. Within the last year, none had lasted more than a couple weeks at most. Not after he so effectively scared them off, one after another. "Uh, not… technically boyfriend, but we're dating."

"Good for you. Where's this one?"

"Home. I mean… here. Knoxville." Roman's cheeks flushed.

Ken raised his eyebrow. "Not *at* home?" When Roman didn't say anything, he laughed. "Well, that's one way to go about it. You didn't chain him to a wall until he said yes to the dress, did you?"

Finally, Roman laughed richly, his cheeks flushing. "Just 'cause I've moved a little fast before…"

"I'm not saying that!" Ken raised his free hand innocently, still wheeling his bag along with the other.

"No, you're right. Mr. Slick… well, hit some bumps," Roman chuckled. "We're figuring things out as we go. I haven't even brought up labels yet. He's had a string of bad luck, so he's been crashing with me while I help him recover from an injury. If he'd actually *sit still* once in a blue moon," he muttered.

"Oh." Ken whistled. "Dude. That's good of you, man."

Roman shrugged it off as they approached the gate, but his mind was effectively back on Oscar.

Something had changed. Not just because of Oscar, but maybe because of what he'd found with him.

The playboy attitude didn't appeal, all of a sudden. He wasn't looking to flash those four gold bars, as Oscar had said, and pick up a pretty thing for a night. Hell, maybe he'd only ever been settling for that before.

If Oscar had taught him anything already, it was that he had to stop settling for what he didn't really want, just because he thought he should want it—in all areas of his life. And right now, staring at the plane he was about to board, it felt like a hell of a lot like settling.

CHAPTER
Nineteen

OSCAR

Two missed calls.

Oscar's heart dropped when he saw Roman's name on the phone notification. He couldn't think what was up, but he didn't like the sound of more than one.

He flicked the silencing switch on his phone and called Roman's number as he unlocked his car.

Straight to voicemail.

That was weird. He knew Roman usually kept his phone on, in case work called him. Maybe he was already on the line.

Or maybe we're going out for drinks with the brothers and I forgot. It was Friday, after all. Even though Roman worked tomorrow night, he could go out, if not drink. But he was sure Roman hadn't mentioned them getting together *this* Friday.

He pulled out his phone again as he was about to release the parking brake and sent Falcon a text. *Is it a bar night this weekend?*

By the time he got to Roman's driveway—Roman's car

not there, he noticed—the phone held an answer. He frowned.

No, why? Falcon had answered.

He didn't respond yet, just grabbed his keys and headed inside. It was probably nothing.

Somehow, he sensed Roman's absence before he saw the note; maybe there was something Roman packed in his case that was missing now. Whatever it was, he glared at the note as though not reading it would change it.

Finally he approached the counter and leaned on it, looking the words over.

"Cocky bastard," he laughed under his breath, pretending the words hadn't stung.

Just off to Singapore, like we're not even a thing. See ya.

Don't be dramatic, he told himself, shaking his head. It was Roman's job, after all. He couldn't very well say no if they needed him. Being called in was part of the job. So were long absences.

Oscar crashed on the couch and pulled one knee up to his chest, hugging it and letting his chin gently thump onto his knee, wrapping his arm around his leg. He had to keep the injured leg loosely straight, or the brace pulled uncomfortably.

After a few moments glumly staring into space, he remembered Falcon's text and gave him a call back.

"Hey. What's up?" Falcon asked.

"Nothing. I just couldn't figure out where Roman was. He got called into work a day early, while I was out."

"Oh! Shit, you need anything while he's gone?"

"I wouldn't mind talking out a crazy idea of mine about this building I just toured after my appointment. But no, I won't starve," Oscar told Falcon, an amused smile tugging his lips.

"Mysterious! If you're sure you're fine," Falcon told him. "Physio went well, at least?"

"Yep. The TENS machine is the best part of my week." Oscar actually wasn't exaggerating that much, either. The electric currents tingling through his knee soothed the muscle, if only for that brief time. "I'm getting one for home."

"Oh, awesome. I bet it'd be great for kinky stuff."

Despite himself, Oscar laughed, uncurling and stretching out. "God, your mind is dirty."

"Like *yours* isn't," Falcon countered. "I know you."

Oscar shushed him. "Anyway, he's still not happy with how fast I'm recovering. The brace is all fine, but I'm supposed to stay off it even more for the next week."

"Sooo, you *do* need me to come over and cook?"

Oscar hesitated for a few long moments, then sighed. "If you *have* to."

"I'm on it," Falcon told him. "And you can tell me about your crazy idea while I bring you… Chinese?"

Oscar breathed a sigh. "God, yes. Did I mention I love you?"

"Get in line." Falcon lowered his voice. "Blane did that, you know, *would you feel okay with one of us proposing to the other sometime in the future*, the generic opening-the-door talk…"

"Oh, shit. No way."

"Yeah way. I dunno, maybe he's planning something for Christmas. Or he's getting permission for whenever, just in case, and I'll be waiting three years," Falcon laughed. "God only knows, with him."

"And… no, I'm delaying you from getting Chinese, which

means I'm keeping Chinese away from *me*. Come over now so I can interrogate you," Oscar ordered him. "And eat."

Falcon laughed. "There's my Oscar. On my way."

"No way." Falcon covered his mouth, at least, when his jaw dropped midway through a bite of Chinese food.

"I know," Oscar laughed. "Me, renting a commercial place. Scary."

Falcon shook his head. "But, wait. Wouldn't that set back your knee?"

"Well…" Oscar grimaced. "It *should* recover without much extra support, when I actually rest it." Falcon's eyes gleamed, and before he could say it, Oscar cut him off. "I know, I know. You told me so. Roman told me so. The fucking world told me so. And if I'd listened, maybe I'd still…"

He cut himself off and stabbed a chicken piece with his chopsticks, then let his breath out in a quick whoosh and ate it.

"Sorry," Falcon murmured. "That's not easy. I have nightmares about what I'll do if I injure my hands."

Oscar's head snapped up as he stared at his best friend. Falcon had never told him that before, but it made perfect sense. "I was always like this. And then it came true, and… I guess the world hasn't ended, but…"

Nothing matched the feeling under the spotlight on stage, doing exactly what he did in practice, and for fun, and often unconsciously as he walked down the street. Watched by thousands but aware of nobody in particular, only the movements that resonated deep within, baring a piece of his soul…

It was impossible to describe without getting emotional, and he'd had enough of that lately. He just sighed and lifted his shoulders. "I miss it. But you'd make it work. I am, somehow."

"So, teaching?"

Oscar nodded. He'd floated his plan, and Falcon hadn't laughed. *Him*, a teacher? But Falcon just looked thoughtful. "I know. I kind of want to… form a company, too. You know, when I have enough students. Obviously not like, a *huge* touring company or anything, but my own thing. Maybe with gay dancers. Actually…"

"What?"

"I know it's the *in thing* now, reinterpretations, but I want to reinterpret a lot of the classics with gay, trans, queer people. *Us*." Oscar leaned in, keenly aware of something stirring in his chest.

He hadn't felt this since… fuck, since the injury. He was excited. Genuine, deep joy filled him at the possibilities lying in front of him. Maybe he couldn't star, but he could create the message—reinvent it, even. Give others the chance to tell *their* stories, not be stuck supporting the same old stories, as many male dancers wound up doing. Lifting pretty ballerinas and looking strong and sensual on stage, like they weren't wrapping their legs around hunky men's waists in their off hours.

Falcon beamed at him. "Well, I think you have your answer. You can start locally. Nashville has a bigger population, if you need it. Or move to a big city when you have a name for yourself."

Oscar surprised himself at his resistance to the idea of moving—after all, he'd spent years basically on the road. But that had been before Roman. It was way too early to plan to leave *or* stay.

"Maybe," he settled on for now. "One thing at a time. I like it here. The climate is good for small businesses. More people I know around here, that kind of thing."

Falcon leaned in. "Man, you looked happy there. I take it back. Wait to heal up so you don't screw yourself up for life—that's important. But you have time, if you're signing a lease. Gives you time to recruit students and advertise, right?"

Oscar relaxed and smiled. With Falcon on board, he could do this. And he had no doubt Roman would support him, when he was home to hear about it.

Before Falcon arrived, he'd sent a quick text to let Roman know that he was fine and had just been out working on a project. The photos he'd attached ought to distract him from asking any questions.

He had a world clock on his phone now with other time zones for Roman's frequent destinations. He had barely taken off, let alone landed, so Falcon expected a response would take a while.

"It's a plan," Oscar found himself nodding. "I don't even rent an *apartment*, let alone a studio," he added with a laugh. "So I might need help with the paperwork."

"Hey, we know people now," Falcon told him with a grin. "Guess who just bought property? We'll help you out." Oscar tried to push himself to his feet, but Falcon glared and stood up to lean down and hug him instead. "Don't you dare."

Oscar laughed into Falcon's shoulder and hugged him tightly back. "It's going to be fabulous, darling."

"Welcome back," Falcon murmured. "It's so good to see you."

CHAPTER

Twenty

ROMAN

"ROMAN, MY MAN!"

And it had almost been a nice flight.

Getting to the gate had revealed why Ken had chosen now to reveal what he knew about Cory: the asshole was their third man on the flight deck today.

Ken had given him an anxious glance, but Roman could feign politeness as well as the next Tennessean. Gentlemen's agreements were how shifts were usually sorted out.

With Ken and Cory working the first shift, Roman had been stuck with a four-hour rest period, which hadn't been very restful. That was why nobody wanted the first sleep period, while they were already wide awake, but he'd agreed to take it on the basis of having the least seniority.

Working with Cory was inevitable. The flight commander was Ken, so Ken was in charge of the takeoff and landing, and signed the flight plan. The middle shift—that was all Roman's.

And Cory was beaming at him as Ken handed over

control of the cabin to him. "Our knight in shining armor. I didn't know they were calling you in."

"Me neither, until they did," Roman said. The dry humor was lost on Cory.

"I'll leave you two to it, then," Ken said pointedly, giving Roman an extra glance. When Roman lied and nodded an *I'm fine* nod, Ken headed out.

Leaving the two of them alone at the controls of a 777 with three hundred people aboard, whose safety Roman immediately put in the forefront of his mind. He busied himself checking the instruments, but that could only take up a few minutes, and Cory was already talking at him.

"Did you see the game last night?"

"Yeah, man. Great game," Roman responded automatically. Cory never seemed to notice that he never had anything to say about said games.

"No kidding! When O'Brien crossed over behind Shaw at the last second for the goal, that was goddamn genius. Like they were using, like, telepathy."

"Mmm."

"And a real overtime win. Jesus. It makes every other game this season look boring as shit. And they are, aren't they? The league was way better when we were growing up, you know? More on the line. All this safety shit these days…"

Hockey, Roman guessed. He nodded and tuned out. The conversation stayed mundane and mind-numbing but unengaging for a good half hour as Cory worked his way through all the sports that had apparently been played recently.

Then the conversation moved to Cory's girlfriends and the desperate measures he'd had to take to keep them finding out about each other. Roman had long ago learned not to judge his coworkers, just listened and offered sympathy without advice or approval.

Then what he was waiting for—the sneaky approach.

"But I bet you don't have those problems, huh?"

Roman looked over at him slowly. It was steady, level flying without any traffic nearby, and not a cloud in sight. No chance of distracting him without being very obvious. He was almost there, but not quite yet.

"What do you mean?"

"Dating guys. We're not all crazy, huh?" Cory grinned.

"Only some of us," Roman muttered, but Cory missed it.

"And, you know, nagging us and checking our phones when we get back from a long flight…"

"Before you have a chance to clear your texts, you mean?" Roman answered, raising an eyebrow.

Cory snickered. "Right."

I feel like I'm talking to a wall. Roman hummed. "Sure. It's fine."

"So, uh, you going out anywhere when we get there?" Cory asked.

Okay, twice? What the fuck. "Man, what's up with you suddenly wanting to integrate into our culture?" Roman asked, casting a suspicious look at him. "It doesn't sound like you liked it last time."

"Oh, it was great. But we could have skipped the whole shebang, you know…"

Roman blankly looked at Cory.

"Come on, we're all guys here. You know. We don't need to get all warmed up, buying each other drinks…"

Roman raised his eyebrow. "Yeah?"

"Is it a date?"

"Just come out and ask what you want, dude. I'm clueless." Not as clueless as he wanted to be, though. Roman was starting to get a suspicion what was going on.

"Well, if you don't wanna bother going into town and all that, any port in a storm…" Cory raised his brows meaningfully. "I got the same needs as you, bro."

"Are you picking me up?"

"I wouldn't say *that*," Cory laughed. "Just an offer, dude. Don't get all uppity."

"You'll kindly let me… what?"

Cory stuck his tongue in his cheek pointedly and then glanced down at himself.

Great, he'll let me suck his dick. Like any old straight guy. Jesus.

"Really? Here, of all places?" Roman stated flatly.

"We can discuss it later if you'd rather, I guess," Cory shrugged carelessly. "But what else is going on?" He gestured around the skies. "And in two hours, the black box will erase all this. Or half an hour, manually."

"I have command. It's *my* call whether to erase those tapes early," Roman stated, his jaw tight.

"Yes, *sir*," Cory smirked, and he managed to make it sound like an innuendo. "I'll submit to your command, of course."

Roman took a deep, calming breath. *I guess we're having it out now. Less than ideal.* He checked all his instruments again, almost hoping for a problem. Not major, of course. Just a little glitch that could distract him for a few minutes.

No such luck.

"You've been getting weird on me ever since I got promoted," Roman started slowly. "Have you been trying to get into my pants?"

"Nah," Cory snorted. "Of course not." He said it with a

disgusted lip curl, like he couldn't quite believe he was doing it himself.

"You're straight. Just curious. Or *willing* to let me treat you, huh?" Roman continued.

Cory paused, eyeing Roman for a moment before lifting his shoulders in a shrug. "I got girlfriends."

"Right. But it's not cheating if it's a guy, huh? On either of them?"

"Cheating? Whoa, man. I didn't say that." Cory put his hands up. "I'm just choosing the girl I got the best shot with. And it's none of their business. Guys will be guys when we're alone, huh?"

"Is my number on the schedule as *for a good time, call*, or something?" Roman snapped, not even bothering to hide his anger.

Cory looked startled. "What? Calm down, man. Nobody has to know about this." Abruptly, his hand was on Roman's thigh. Warm pressure from each of his fingers crawled up Roman's skin.

Roman whirled on him and glared so fiercely Cory's seat rocked as he recoiled. "Don't you fucking touch me again, you fucking creep. We. Are. At. Work."

Cory flatly watched him, his cheeks reddening as he folded his arms tightly.

"There are three hundred people on board this plane, and *we* are the only two people in charge of getting them to the ground. *After* we land, and we're off work, you can make any indecent proposals you still wanna make to me. Or call one of your girlfriends, tell her about the other, and jerk it by yourself in the shower like a decent fucking human being. Got it?"

Cory snorted and shrugged carelessly. "Suit yourself." His

casual words were at odds with his quick breathing and the tight muscles in his body.

But, for the first time ever, there was silence in the cockpit for five minutes. It stretched to ten, then fifteen before Roman finally felt the adrenaline ebbing.

It was gonna be a long few hours, but for being so hard-won, the silence was the most peaceful he'd ever had.

CHAPTER

Twenty~One

OSCAR

Not a good time to talk. I'll call in an hour?

Oscar nearly jumped when his phone went off with Roman's ringtone and then showed him the befuddling message first thing in the morning. He'd just poured milk into his breakfast cereal, and the sexts he'd sent Roman last night were the last thing on his mind.

Slowly, with the help of the coffee he'd half-drained, his brain woke up. "Oh, boy."

Roman had better not be mad at him for leaving the house without talking to him. It hadn't been the best idea, Oscar would admit, but he hadn't known Roman might just suddenly disappear to Hong Kong or wherever.

Opting for simplicity for now, he sent a quick text back: *Hope everything's OK. Call me when you can.*

Will do. The two-word response didn't assuage any of his fears.

Too busy staring at his phone and imagining the best way to respond to imaginary verbal attacks by Roman for his sloppiness and carelessness in leaving the house without telling him, Oscar only remembered his cereal after it was soggy. He sighed and started eating it anyway, since he had a goddamn hour to fill.

Then he grabbed his crutches, the stupid fucking things that he'd been prescribed—at a rather unaffordable price, except if he compared it to his long-term health and mobility —and made his way to the couch.

Not being able to pace back and forth as he waited nearly drove him mad, and when the call came in, he answered on the first ring with a sigh of relief.

"Roman. Hey."

"Hi, hon. How's it going?" Roman sounded tired. Didn't they sleep on the flight? When Oscar asked as much, though, Roman just chuckled. "Didn't get much sleep, no. I had first shift in the coffin."

"The *coffin?*" Oscar's voice squeaked.

Roman laughed, sounding a little more awake now. "Sorry. Sleeping bunks."

"That's… creative." Oscar shook his head. "Anyway. Why was it a bad time? What's going on?"

Roman's sigh crackled through the phone, and then he said, "Can we video call?"

"Yeah, of course." Oscar fiddled with his phone and hit the video camera button, hastily touching his hair as the camera came on.

Roman appeared at about the same time, in an old t-shirt he sometimes wore to bed and propped up against what looked like a hotel headboard. "Hey there. You're looking perky."

Oscar raised the coffee mug into the frame. "I thought about bringing the coffee pot over here so I don't have to get up and use my crutches—they're making me use them this week, by the way."

"Shit," Roman winced. "Because you won't sit still?"

"Yeah, yeah," Oscar rolled his eyes. "Because I won't sit still. Says the man in Hong Kong."

Roman laughed. "Ouch. True. Uh, by the way..." His expression was worried. "Sorry I had to leave so fast."

"No, it's work. I get it," Oscar assured him. "Sorry I wasn't around."

"Okay, it's cool."

"Cool." There was an awkward moment as they looked at their phone screens, not quite at each other. Oscar didn't want to make this a big deal, especially with something else going on. Then, he added, "So, you wanna talk about it, or...?"

"Oh! Yeah. Uh, it's nothing. Bad day at work."

Oscar's chest tightened. *When he says that, it could mean an engine caught fire.* "Everything fine?"

"Yes. Yeah, fine. Just coworkers."

Roman seemed like he was dancing around something, so Oscar let it go. Instead, he offered, "Uh, so, I was out because I've been touring some studios nearby."

"Oh." Roman blinked a few times. "Studios like... dance?"

"That's the one. I'm still no good with a brush. Falcon's tried, believe me."

Roman chuckled. "I bet he has. So, are you going to tell me?"

There was still an awkwardness between them, and Oscar tried not to let it get to him. They hadn't had a chance to say goodbye, after all, and they were now something stupid like twelve hours apart. And through a digital screen? Of course it was weird.

"Well, I thought I'd open my own studio after this has

healed up. Teach people. Then start a company, eventually. Long-term plans, but I'll start small and affordable," Oscar half-smiled. "At least, affordable as long as I can keep rent down."

"Right, right. That sounds great. Are you thinking of… a studio with like, a living space? Or staying with me?" Roman looked anxious. "I hope I haven't made you feel unwelcome. Hardly being home and all."

"Jesus," Oscar laughed, rolling his eyes. "If you made me feel any more welcome there'd be a freaking red carpet. Don't worry, man."

He could sense the ice breaking between them, and Roman laughed. "Okay. But really, what are you thinking?"

"Well," Oscar hummed. "I haven't dated anyone I've lived with before."

"Me neither. Then again, I barely live anywhere, it feels like. Someone may as well use the damn house, you know?"

Oscar nodded, recalling overhearing his end of the conversation about switching to short-hauls. "It's not the usual way to start dating. But nothing about this has been typical so far."

Roman chuckled. "I think nothing about us is typical." He paused, gazing at the camera for a moment, then sighed. "I should tell you. One of my coworkers tried to pick me up today."

"Oh." Oscar blinked a few times. "If he's cute and you don't invite him home, I don't care."

Roman stared. "Wait, what?"

"What do you… I mean… wait, do you want us to be…" Oscar trailed off. They'd only barely agreed to start dating, let alone exclusive. Was this a boyfriend thing? He gulped.

"I, uh," Roman laughed, rubbing his neck. He was blushing. "I'm cool with that kind of thing, but to be honest, I don't want anyone else right now. It's been weird to realize that, but it's true. And if I'm on short-hauls, I see you nearly every night…"

Oscar tried not to squirm or let on the glow that was building in his chest. "You want to come home to me?"

"Yes." Roman didn't hesitate to answer.

"Well, um." Oscar was blushing too—he could feel his face getting hot. He tried not to look at the picture in the corner of the screen that showed him his own face, because it would only make him blush harder. "Cool. That's, um, yeah. Aren't we the awkwardest?"

Roman laughed and rubbed his face. "We are. I'm sorry. All that slickness just… I can't pretend around you." It perhaps was the most unguarded thing he'd said, and he seemed to realize it, too. His eyes widened. "I mean, I don't want to rush you—"

"No," Oscar interrupted. He was absolutely glowing now, despite his attempt to hide it. "No, I'm glad you're so into me. It actually feels kind of nice. I don't feel so…" he trailed off, searching for a word. *Broken* wasn't it, but it was close. "Ineffectual? I don't know. When you have this one job and it's what you've trained all your life for, and then it's just gone…"

"A lot of pilots who get disability, get in accidents, get fired for whatever reason… it's like that for them, too," Roman assured him, his voice somber. "I understand. It hasn't happened to me, but buddies of mine, yeah. Most pilots are straight outta high school, no kind of career prospects otherwise."

Oscar breathed out quietly and nodded. "That's why I'm teaching. Not just because I like teaching people—I don't know if I will yet. I do, from the workshops we've led on the road. Full-time? I don't know. But it's *something*. And I feel useless if I sit around doing nothing."

"See, that's what I like about you," Roman said with a small but warm smile. "Even if it bugs the crap out of me that you can't sit still for a couple weeks, you've got a work ethic like nobody else. Well, maybe Blane, but his job is way more nine-to-five."

"Except when he has kangaroos in the kitchen."

Roman laughed richly, and the sound made Oscar grin, even coming through the speaker from thousands of miles away. "Lemurs in the living room."

"Baboons in the bedroom. Wait, I don't want to think about that…" Oscar wrinkled his nose. He'd walked in on Falcon and some hookup a couple times, which was a couple times too many.

Roman laughed again, even longer this time. When he caught his breath, his cheeks red, he gazed at the phone. "Man, I know it's awfully early, but I reckon you know already. I really like you, you know? It's—this—this is nice. Just nice," he finished, then gave Oscar a pleading look as if begging him not to laugh.

Oscar stifled it to a quiet giggle. "I like you too, baby." Something was niggling at the corner of his mind, though. "Hon, you know what you said earlier?"

"Which bit?" Roman winked. "The bit about coming home to you? You never answered, really."

"I'll keep living with you." Oscar raised his finger. "Only if you agree to cook me supper sometimes, when you're home. I like your cooking."

Roman smiled. "You do? It's not great."

"It's fine," Oscar told him firmly. "You know all I can do is coffee. But I'm working on it. I stopped by the library and got a cookbook."

Roman laughed. "No way."

"Yeah way. I'll be able to make scrambled eggs by the time you get back." Oscar winked. "Maybe even toast."

"Don't burn the house down while I'm gone," Roman pled. "I don't know how my home insurance would take it."

Oscar mimicked a phone call by holding his thumb to his ear, pinky against his lips. He deepened his voice to imitate Roman. "Yeah, hi, I'm in Singapore, and my live-in boyfriend just burned down the house making toast. Can I start a claim?"

Roman raised his eyebrows. "So, boyfriends?"

"Um." Oscar cleared his throat and chewed his lip. "If you… I mean, you only want me…"

"I didn't want to push you into being exclusive, *or* long-term, before you were ready." Roman took a breath as if considering whether he should admit it, then plunged ahead. "I've been fucking *dying* to ask you, though."

Oscar laughed gently. "I won't judge you for wanting to seal the deal. I *am* pretty great, some hot guy once told me. Not long ago."

"Mmm. Will you ditch him to be with me?" Roman winked.

"I'm sleeping in his bed. It could get awkward." Oscar glanced toward the guest room. "Or actually, his guest room."

"Take my bed. Keep it warm while I'm gone." Roman cleared his throat, then added, "I mean, if you want."

Oscar beamed back at him. "Yeah, I want." Roman's eyes were nearly drooping shut, so he added, "Get some rest, baby. You look wiped. Call me in the morning while I'm going to bed."

"Okay." Roman kissed his fingers and waved at the camera, and Oscar had to fight the urge to squeal. His heart felt so full it was bursting.

"Miss you." Oscar cleared his throat and waved.

"Miss you too. Have a good day."

"Have a good night," Oscar countered, his finger shaking as he hit the *hang up* button. He put down his phone and covered his face as his chest tightened and throbbed with joy.

He wants me. He really, actually wants me.

Today was the best day ever, except for one minor detail: Falcon was coming over in an hour to clean and hang out with him, and he'd forgotten to ask if they were going to tell them yet.

"Shit. I'm never gonna make it," Oscar groaned, closing his eyes as he laughed.

And the text message he got a moment later? It didn't help matters.

I'm on my way over to make lunch. Don't you dare move that leg of yours. PS: the brothers are all going out tonight.

Oscar tapped out a text to Roman: *If the guys find out, is that OK?* But Roman had already gone offline, and it was clear within a couple minutes that he wasn't coming back.

"I'm fucked."

CHAPTER
Twenty~Two

OSCAR

"Hey, relax, man." Falcon slapped Oscar's good knee. "You look like you're about to jump out of the car. You've met them all before. They're not gonna bite your head off."

Oscar offered Falcon a quick smile. "Yeah, of course. Sorry. Just lots on my mind."

Falcon eyed him critically across the backseat of their Uber. They'd already discussed Oscar's studio a little more, and Falcon's hunch that Blane was going to propose, and just about everything Oscar could think of that wasn't related to Roman.

Which left an awkward and very obvious silence between them.

Falcon knew him well enough to leave well enough alone when he wasn't ready to talk, but he was giving Oscar the look that meant he knew something was up.

"It's nothing," Oscar mumbled, looking out the window. Why did his new boyfriend have to live so far out in the freaking suburbs? Like a white-picket-fence guy. Which he was.

He couldn't believe he was dating a white-picket-fence guy. Hell, he couldn't believe he was dating any guy. Let alone his best friend's boyfriend's best friend. Like some weird little dating club.

"Uh huh. Nothing," Falcon repeated, his lips twitching upward in amusement. "I believe you."

"I don't wanna talk about it."

"I gathered, because you're not talking about it."

"I'm not saying."

"I'm not asking."

Oscar stared out the window, his cheeks burning. "Good."

"But the other guys won't have a problem asking." Falcon was smirking at him.

Oscar looked over and rolled his eyes. "Asshole."

"I know. So?"

"There might be… a thing going on."

Falcon burst out laughing. "Wow. So specific. I'm very glad I asked. I'll run to the tabloids now."

"Fuck off."

Still laughing, Falcon covered his mouth and looked away, desperately trying to regain composure.

Unable to help himself, Oscar joined in the laughter. "Fine, fine, all right. Jesus. I'm kinda seeing someone."

"Nooooo." Falcon couldn't have been more sarcastic if he'd tried. "Really? I had *no* idea."

"Fuck *off.*"

Even the Uber driver made a stifled sound of amusement.

"Okay, don't tell me more," Falcon answered with a wry smile. "Keep blushing every time I say Roman's name. Oh… there you go again."

Oscar's cheeks were hot at Falcon's words. *Oh, for fuck's sake. Does everyone know?* "Whatever."

"I haven't told them. And Blane hasn't noticed. Some-times I wonder if he'd notice me trying to propose to him," Falcon laughed. "I'd have to get a skywriter. But like I said, I'm just waiting for him instead. Much easier than repeating some long *marry me* speech when he just stares at me."

Oscar relaxed slightly and chuckled at the mental image. "You think he'd be that surprised?"

"Oh, yeah." Falcon winked. "But some of the others are more, uh… perceptive. Nico and Deen will be all over you."

"Fuck. I haven't asked him what to say." Oscar glanced out the window as he frowned. "It's nearly morning there, and this all so new to us…"

"Then don't give them the whole scoop. If anyone asks you when to expect wedding bells, I'll kick him in the nuts for you," Falcon offered cheerily. "But you better not with-hold on *me*."

"I thought you…" Oscar trailed off, then shifted uncom-fortably.

Falcon waited, eyebrow raised. "Hm?"

No getting out of it now. Oscar wasn't sure how his best friend in the world would take it. "I thought you'd judge us."

Falcon paused for a few long moments, then squinted at him. "Huh? Judge you? Why the hell's that?"

"You and Blane didn't want us getting together. You've been trying to keep Roman and me apart since the start, you know," Oscar said, trying not to make it sound like an accu-sation. But now that he was talking, something was unknot-ting in his chest, like a burden he hadn't even admitted to himself. "It's like you don't trust us to date like adults."

"I… guess we were," Falcon said slowly, rubbing his fore-head. "At the beginning for sure. I mean, you've both been a little… how do I put it…"

"Slutty?"

Falcon laughed. "Sure, but I meant *love him and leave him*."

"So, slutty," Oscar grinned. "I cop to it. It's fun."

"But now that there's you and Roman...?" Falcon prompted, clearly curious.

Oscar felt his cheeks flush again. It sounded so stupidly romantic in his head. "We talked a bit about it. Like I said, really new. We both think we only want to see each other. There's room to talk about things in the future, and stuff, and whatever..." he waved a hand, then bit his tongue. He was in serious danger of rambling now. "But I guess we're officially boyfriends. And stuff."

Falcon was beaming at him when he finally dared to glance over. "That's adorable. I like seeing you in this stage. You usually don't sound so optimistic, though."

Oscar drew a breath to protest, then let it out. "I guess not." His usual attitude was *we'll see how long it lasts*, and he was usually right, because he'd had a whole life that wasn't compatible with dating outside the company, and dating inside the company was an even worse idea.

"No pressure," Falcon added and punched his shoulder lightly. "But man, that's cool for you. If it's anything like what I found with Blane..." he trailed off. It was his turn to look embarrassed.

"Hm?" Oscar teased. "What's this mushy stuff?"

"Fuck off. You know I love him. Having him around just makes me feel like I'm... I don't know. Vibrating at a higher frequency or something."

"Vibrating?" Oscar grinned as the Uber pulled up outside the bar. "No, I don't wanna know." He leaned forward and thanked the driver, then stepped out.

Falcon snorted as he joined Oscar on the sidewalk and

shut the car door. "You know, they make great long-distance ones now."

"Oh, I know." It wasn't the first time the thought had occurred to Oscar. "But he might switch around his shifts for… more evenings at home. Go to short-hauls."

Falcon's brows shot up. "Oh. He's serious."

Something lurched in Oscar's chest: fear? Anxiety? He wasn't sure what it was, exactly, but it was unsettling to hear that Roman *was* pursuing him seriously. "We're trying to take it slowly," he answered, avoiding Falcon's gaze.

Thankfully, Josh was just walking down the block toward them. He raised his arm in an enthusiastic wave. "Hey, guys!"

Falcon gazed at Oscar for a moment longer, making it clear the conversation wasn't over, then looked back at Josh. "Hey! At least we're not the last here, huh?"

"Shut up. I had errands. Forgot the time," Josh grumbled, rolling his eyes. He was ruddy-cheeked and out of breath, and his overshirt was the kind of plaid monstrosity that came straight from his farm wardrobe rather than the clean but plain t-shirts he seemed to favor otherwise.

"Hot Grindr date kept you busy?" Falcon teased, noticing the same things but having more license to tease their friend.

Josh flipped Falcon off and pulled open the door. "After you."

"Enjoy the view," Falcon countered and sauntered through, towing Oscar after him. "But the goods are taken."

"Wait a minute," Josh said when he caught up with them in the middle of the bar. "Is there another boyfriend on the scene? Oscar's? Why isn't he here?" He looked between Oscar and Falcon.

"For you all to terrify?" Falcon laughed. "Give the man a break."

"I hope you realize he'll have to pass the test with us," Josh told Oscar, elbowing him but grinning. "Good for you. Gonna spill?"

Oscar glared at Falcon. "You could have kept a secret for more than three seconds, you know."

Josh laughed. "Don't blame him. It was my nosiness." He gave them that broad boyish smile, looking every inch the easygoing country boy. He might attract some attention tonight, if he were lucky. From someone who didn't mind plaid and faded denim.

Man, I picked the right brother. Oscar resisted the urge to laugh to himself as he approached the table with the others and raised a hand to wave. He still felt a bit shy around them, but they'd welcomed him in so thoroughly that it wasn't bad.

And, apparently, they were intrigued by his love life as much as the others'. Josh said loudly, "I'm buying this round so we can get Oscar drunk and interrogate him on this mysterious new man in his life."

A round of *oooh*s went around, and Oscar groaned as he shut his eyes.

I was right. Totally fucked.

Through skillful subject changes, strategic silences, and pleading looks at Falcon, Oscar made it about an hour into the get-together before the attention turned to him.

He'd spent the last hour mentally preparing for how to brush off questions truthfully but without implicating Roman, but he wasn't prepared for Nico to lean over the table and drop the grenade.

"So, you and Roman shacked up respectably yet? Or are you still living in sin?"

Deen burst out laughing and slapped Nico's chest. "Don't scare off the poor guy."

Josh nearly dropped his beer. "*Ohhhh.*"

Blane stared at Falcon. "What? Really? I didn't—what?"

"It's a good thing you're cute," Falcon told him with a head shake. "You didn't figure it out last time they visited?"

Even Dustin was smiling to himself, not commenting but also not dissuading them from this line of questioning.

"Is it Roman?" Tyler pressed, never one for subtlety or unanswered questions.

All eyes were on Oscar, who groaned and looked at Falcon.

His best friend winked. "Hey, don't look at me. They figured it out on their own. My lips have been sealed. Unlike yours."

A roar of laughter went around the table.

"Et tu?" Oscar couldn't help laughing, even though he kind of wanted to disappear into the floor. "Jesus."

"If he doesn't wanna talk, it's fine. We'll just grill Roman next," Tyler cheerily continued. "We can break him a lot faster."

Oscar laughed again, a hand over his face. His cheeks were roasting. "Fucking... okay, fine." *Bare details.* "We're still figuring it out."

"All the benefits, none of the responsibility?" Josh grinned.

Falcon winked. "You're one to talk."

"Hey," Josh elbowed Falcon. "We're not talking about me."

Dustin snuck a word in edgewise. "We've never gone this

long without Roman hinting at his next conquest, you know. It was pretty obvious."

"Was it?" Blane said, still looking dazed. "He never said…"

"Of course he didn't say. He *likes* him. When does that ever happen?" Josh muttered under his breath.

Someone hummed a few beats of the wedding tune, to more laughter.

Okay. That's kind of overwhelming. Being the one *for him or whatever.* Yet Oscar was trying hard not to beam as he heard this. "Fine. We both, uh, kind of stumbled into each other. So it's still really new. We're boyfriends, but we haven't even agreed to tell you guys yet. If you can give me a chance to get there first when he wakes up…" He checked his phone: late enough that he was awake now. "Tonight. Or until his flight back tomorrow."

Nico groaned. "No teasing group texts? Fine."

"I was going to give him a *congratulations, about fucking time* card," Josh chimed in.

Falcon flapped a hand at them all, finally jumping in to rescue him. "Okay, enough gossip. Before Oscar dies of embarrassment. He looks like he's trying to camouflage himself in a tomato field."

"You're a good sport," Josh assured Oscar with a warm smile and slapped his back. "Sorry we're nosy asses. Another beer? It's on me."

"I'll take one," Tyler told him.

"I wasn't offering you. Unless you have juicy gossip for us."

Tyler looked disappointed. "No. Goddammit."

"Stick your dick in something other than one of those supercars and report back, I'll buy you a beer," Josh told him.

"Hell, figure out how to stick your dick in a supercar and I'll buy you two."

Deen looked thoughtful. "You know, I once saw this video…"

"Don't give him any ideas," Dustin hissed. "You know how many guys end up in the ER with their junk stuck in things?"

Oscar stared, horrified. "I wanna know how *you* know. It's not like you need a forensics expert to figure out whose dick is stuck in the fence…"

They all winced with reflexive pain.

Dustin snorted with laughter. "Friends in high places. I have this buddy who's a nurse. He's seen things, man."

Josh slid out of the booth, squeezing across Nico and Deen's laps to do so. "Is he going to tell that story again? We're all gonna need more alcohol for this conversation." He headed for the bar.

Oscar held his breath, but he could tell the group was waiting for him to ask. If this was the worst hazing got, he could deal with it. *The things I do for friends.* "Okay, I'll bite. What story?"

"An unlucky, lonely bastard plus a pool intake valve and several firefighters."

Oscar winced and covered his groin for a second. "Okay, Josh was right. I will need beer for this one."

There was another round of laughter, but now that the attention wasn't on him, he joined in. He was proud that he'd navigated that kind of smoothly—the best he could under the circumstances, anyway.

Now to hope that Roman wasn't pissed off at him tomorrow morning.

CHAPTER
Twenty~Three
ROMAN

GOING TO BED. YOUR BROS GOT ME SO DRUNK. THEY KNOW ABOUT us. xoxo

Roman rubbed the sleep out of his eyes and slowly pushed himself to sit upright, staring at the screen of his phone. That text was half an hour ago. No way would Oscar still be awake.

"Oh, Jesus," he muttered and tossed his phone on the bed. No calls from his brothers yet, but he had no doubt they were coming.

So much for keeping it secret. He should have known, really—nothing got past them for long. He couldn't blame Oscar for divulging when he didn't know what had even been said. Maybe all they knew was that they'd hooked up. No way could he fool even himself into thinking that, though. He rejected the idea and tried to come to terms with the fact that they all knew now.

But they *were* his brothers. What was he so nervous about?

Hitting the gym didn't give Roman any answers. It was

soothing to burn off the nervous energy he'd awoken with, but by the time he was back in his hotel room and showering, he still hadn't figured it out.

It was a lifestyle change, but not one that would surprise them—they'd known about his ill-fated dating attempts for years.

Was it because the stakes were higher? Because he really *did* like Oscar, and he wanted Oscar to stick around but wasn't sure how to keep him there?

Moping and thinking was bad for his mental health, so once he'd changed into clean clothes, he set off for a brisk walk around the city.

He tried to keep his mind blank like he did at work sometimes, focusing just on what he saw, heard, and most of all, smelled. Finally, his concentration was rattled.

"Something for your girlfriend?"

Roman blinked and glanced over at the tourist trap owner. He'd largely learned to tune out local sellers. But he *was* casually keeping an eye out for something to bring his new boyfriend to make up for having to leave so suddenly. Plus, Christmas gifts.

"Maybe," he answered, lips tugging into an amused smile. He didn't share what was so amusing as he stepped into the shop and scanned the usual racks of shot glasses, postcards, and sunglasses that were ubiquitous worldwide.

"Orchid perfumes. National flower of Singapore!" The owner was bragging about the display rack near the register, but Roman shook his head.

Biting back a laugh, Roman told him, "Not really a flower kind of girl." He could see the seller moving for the necklace cabinet already, and he shook his head. "I'll just have a look around," he added firmly.

Merlion salt and pepper shakers? It made him laugh as he picked the set up and turned them over in his hands. They were classy but quirky—a lot like Oscar, really. He could see him liking these. And they weren't too personal, either. He wasn't sure if Oscar even wore jewelry.

Goddamn, he needed to get to know his boyfriend better.

"Oh, she cooks a lot?"

Roman bit his tongue before he could correct him. It was all too easy to pretend he was back home, where being gay was legal. *There's another argument in favor of short-hauls.* "Learning to," was all he said as he handed over cash and escaped. "Keep the change."

As he strode around the now-familiar city blocks near the usual crew hotel, Roman's mind turned over everything. Normally, he might party with the rest of the crew and then head out to find a guy—carefully in some places, more openly in others.

Was he going to be a boring family man now?

Even Christmas shopping couldn't distract him that much, and finally he had to admit it was time to head back to the hotel.

"Roman!"

"Huh?" As he entered the hotel lobby, he turned his head to find the source. "Oh, hey."

Ashley, one of the flight attendants, had her slick blond hair pulled back in a bun, but the way she was dressed—even if not in uniform—was unmistakably cabin crew. The hotel staff knew all of them by now, and in return, they tried not to party too hard in the hotel bar. But it looked like they were starting early today.

"Lunch at the grill?" She pointed at the restaurant.

"Sure. Everyone else already there?"

"You know it." She flashed him a grin. "Almost everyone. Cory went straight for the bars."

Good. Cory didn't tend to hang out with the rest of them anyway, but Roman wasn't sure he wouldn't punch the guy if he had to see him before he showed up at the airport tomorrow. He held up his bag. "Thanks. Be there in a minute. Save me a seat?" he asked, and headed for the elevator.

A few minutes later, in a fresh shirt and added light sweater to deal with the incessant A/C in the hotel, he joined the rest of the group.

"There you are!" Ken beamed and waved him over to an empty stool at the hotel bar. "How you doing, man?"

He was being a little over-friendly, as was everyone. Roman almost cringed as he realized what this meant— everyone knew about the little incident with Cory, or some version of events that might or might not resemble reality. Gossip didn't stay secret for long, even on a 777.

"Fine, fine," Roman waved him off. "What's on tap?"

"The usual, plus some cheap local lager on the guest tap today. It's actually not half-bad."

"I'll take that, then."

A pint later, he was at least feeling more relaxed. Two pints and he was chatting to them like the old friends they were, though everyone carefully avoided the subject of what had happened yesterday.

Tomorrow night's flight was… well, tomorrow night. He could worry about that later, he told himself.

Which worked very well until someone slapped him on the back just as he was taking a drink and said, "Decided you're not too good for us, huh?"

After the coughing and choking was over with, Roman

narrowed his eyes to the hardest expression he could muster as he stared back.

"Cory!" Ken's tone sounded false even to Roman's ears. "Uh, what's up?"

"Just came to see what's hanging." Cory's eyes remained fixed on Roman for a few more moments. "Apparently, Roman. Or he could be," he added in a mutter under his breath.

Roman stood up fast. "What does that mean?"

Ken and Derek were getting up too, and Mandy had her hand on Roman's back as if to calm him down.

They were all trained in de-escalation. Of course the crew were trying to help, but Roman didn't want to be brushed off.

"No, I want him to tell me what that means."

Ken mildly commented, "I was wondering that, too."

Cory looked less brave all of a sudden. "It's just a joke, guys. Jesus. Lighten up."

"A joke about what?" Mandy piped up, her hand still on Roman's back. The touch, instead of being annoying, was suddenly calming. *They're not siding with him,* he realized. *Not to use his vile comparison, but they're giving him enough rope to hang himself with.*

"It's a guy thing."

"Uh huh. Not a *Singaporean law* thing," Roman retorted, keeping his voice low. Foreigners weren't usually caught up in the anti-gay bullshit, but there was no sense in tempting fate.

"No," Cory drawled, rolling his eyes. "Jesus. Paranoid much?" He looked like he wanted to say something else.

"Go on," Roman said, folding his arms and standing

straight. At his size and build, he could resemble a brick wall when he wanted to.

"I was gonna ask what you're on, but apparently we're politically correct today."

"Because half the straights around here don't party with that stuff?" Roman snorted. "Get your bigoted ass out of here."

"I think you'd better bring the party somewhere else." That was Ken, quiet but authoritative. And they might technically be equal ranks, but Ken had a hell of a lot more seniority—and a good name.

Cory was clearly thinking the same thing, because he scoffed and strode for the lobby, muttering under his breath.

The collective exhale when he was out of sight was audible.

"You all right, sweetie?" Ashley tried to hug him, and Roman chuckled as he gave her a half-hug. She had always kept an extra eye out for him, often sneaking extra snacks to him when he passed.

"Fine, hon. Thank you." Roman cleared his throat and nodded slightly at Ken as everyone sat down again.

Well, the vibe was shattered now. A few seconds of silence drove that point home.

"Sorry, guys," Roman tried to say, but he was cut off immediately by a chorus of "no"s.

"Not your fault." Derek met his gaze squarely. Roman hadn't interacted with him much, but his gaydar had always pinged.

Suddenly, something deep in his gut lurched. *How many others is he being a dick to? Who don't have equal rank?* "Jesus. I didn't know he'd do that in public."

"Is he like that all the time? I mean, I've heard bits and pieces..." Ken trailed off.

Roman shrugged it off. "Nah, he can be... I mean, he *was* okay."

"You haven't talked to anyone, have you?" Derek said quietly, drawing Roman's eye.

Roman shrugged. "Nah. You know, guys. Hazing."

"I don't know what kind of fly-by-night airline you think you're working for, but that shit is not cool at our airline," Ken said vehemently. "That goes beyond a friendly joke."

"Seriously," Ashley murmured. When Roman looked around, the rest of them were nodding, too.

"Oh." Roman couldn't think of much else to say. "I mean, I'm transferring to short-haul soon, if I can."

"What? Why?" Mandy looked genuinely disappointed. "Is it the beer selection?"

At last, Roman managed a chuckle and squeezed her shoulder appreciatively. "Just fixing up my home life."

"To live with...?" Ken prompted, giving him a mischievous smile.

"The guy on your phone background?" Mandy prompted.

Roman could feel himself turning red before they even started laughing. He'd taken a selfie of himself and Oscar while they were watching movies to send the brothers on their group chat. It had become his phone background sometime last week.

"Yeah." Roman glanced around, but the bartender was busy flirting with a waitress at the service end. He relaxed and glanced back at their little group. Even the flight crew he didn't know as well were smiling. "It's pretty new, but it's... cool. He's living with me."

Mandy nearly dropped her pint glass. "What?"

"God." He laughed and glanced at Ken.

"Don't look at me for backup. You put your own foot in your mouth there," Ken raised his hands.

Roman sighed and tried to briefly summarize it. "He got injured, needed a place to stay, I have a guest room. Now he's just sorta living with me."

"And Cory's jealous."

Roman stared at Mandy for even suggesting it. "What?"

"He's pretty oblivious, isn't he?" she asked one of the new girls, whose name Roman hadn't caught. "Men."

Roman shook his head. "I don't know. I wondered at first, but… I think he's just being a dick at this point."

"Whatever the reason, something has to happen," Ken said firmly, catching Roman's eye. "It's not just off the clock —as if that would be right," he scoffed. "And if this hadn't happened, he could have kept on going. God knows what he might have done. Fistfight in the cabin? That would make headlines."

Roman almost cringed. Running to the teacher to tell had never been his strong point. He preferred intimidating the assholes until they realized they were just scared as shit and trying to lash out first.

"I guess," he mumbled. "I'll deal with it back home."

"Whatever you need—witnesses or anything—we're here," Derek told him.

"That calls for another round. My round," Ken told them, and Roman drew a breath of relief as the subject was dropped.

For now.

Twenty~Four

ROMAN

"You're too tired to drive, aren't you?"

Roman stared at his phone, trying to make his brain work better. Blane sounded like he was giving him a hint. "Uh…" was his eloquent response.

"That's what I thought. I'm outside in the parking lot."

Roman squinted. "What?"

"To pick you up. And get your advice. And kick your ass over *something* you weren't saying."

Suddenly, everything clicked into place. And it was honestly nice to have a break from the routine of arriving home, assessing how tired he was, and climbing in his car for the drive back to the suburbs.

Or grabbing a taxi to a downtown hotel with a swanky king-sized bed and a jacuzzi tub. But strangely, considering how little time had passed since his now-boyfriend had moved in with him, that felt like a lifetime ago. In a good way.

Roman realized he hadn't answered. "Oh! Oh, uh, yeah. Sure. I'll find you, gimme a few minutes."

"I'll be here." Blane hung up, leaving Roman to find his way to the parking lot.

When he swung himself into Blane's car, his friend just about jumped out of his skin.

"Jesus! Didn't even see you there," Blane exclaimed, hastily pocketing his phone.

"Too busy sexting your boyfriend, huh?" Roman grinned.

"Fuck off," Blane told him, but there was a flush of color in his cheeks that told Roman he was right. "Those in glass houses."

"Ah. Yeah. So, this advice," Roman said as he buckled up.

Blane laughed. "That's the least subtle thing I've heard you say—"

"Yeah, whatever."

"And I've heard some whoppers," Blane persisted.

"The advice? Before I fall asleep and forget how to give it?"

Blane cleared his throat and checked all points in his mirror as he backed out. He made a production of joining the road, too. By the time he looked over at Roman, Roman was staring pointedly at him.

"All right, all right." Blane cracked. He patted his pocket. "I got a ring. I'm ready. I'm going to propose to him."

"Your boyfriend and not mine, I hope," Roman deadpanned.

Blane drew half a breath. "It's not funny!" His voice nearly cracked. "This is a once-in-a-lifetime thing..."

"Yeah, yeah," Roman teased, patting his shoulder. "Just pulling your leg. Jesus. You're touchy today."

"I want it to be *right*," Blane breathed out, recovering his composure. He wasn't easily rattled, either. You couldn't have unsteady nerves as a zoo vet—dealing with huge, touchy animals, you had to project calm confidence. It was one reason Blane and Roman got on so well: their jobs had trained them each to be cool under pressure. Yet the thought of proposing had Blane shaken? Oh, true love.

Roman shook his head. "He'll say yes no matter how you ask."

"What? Are you sure?"

"You already, like, pre-proposed, didn't you? And he wants to get engaged?" Roman patiently asked.

Blane winced. "Yeah, good point. Yes. But..."

"Cold feet are for altars, not engagements," Roman sagely told him, then cracked up at the glare his best friend gave him. "Sorry. Uh." He schooled his expression. "He loves you, you love him. It's not cold-calling. Close the sale."

Blane burst out laughing. "Okay, never become a counsellor. Or a doctor. Anyone in a helping profession."

Roman joined in the laughter. "What? I'm very comforting."

"Fuckhead," Blane muttered and punched his shoulder.

Roman shoved him in return.

"Well, if you aren't gonna give advice about *me*..."

Suddenly, the tables were turned. Roman gulped. "Uh, I mean, if you wanna go over your plans..."

"Nah uh uh." Blane slapped his arm. "No, you've earned no mercy from me today. You're dating your live-in guest and my boyfriend's best friend in the world and you forgot to mention this to me... why?"

"This is, like, the third interrogation in as many days," Roman grumbled.

"But most important, I hope."

"Yeah, I suppose." Roman was tapping his toe on the car floor—a nervous habit he'd long since drilled out of himself in the cockpit. "I'm sorry. I just... liked him, and I figured you'd all think he was just another fling. *I* thought he was, at first."

Blane's lips quirked. "Yeah. I know the feeling. But dude, we're not gonna get in your way. You're a motherfucking adult."

"Still don't believe you there," Roman chuckled. "But sure."

Blane grinned. "Yeah, I feel like someone gave us the keys to adulthood, and then ran away, cackling."

"Yeah!" Roman shook his head. "And then we're suddenly figuring out all this stuff: friends, relationships, jobs... everything at once. Failing forward."

Blane patted his shoulder. "At least you're steady on the job front."

"Right. Uh, about that..." Roman cringed. "But Oscar first."

"Oscar first," Blane agreed, his brows furrowing. "I like him. He's good for you. You've settled down a lot in the last month."

"Have I?"

"Normally I'd have learned and forgotten a couple soul-mates' names now," Blane teased.

"Was I *that* bad?" Roman exclaimed.

Blane hummed noncommittally, which meant *yes*. "It's nice to see you happy, that's all. Remember when you were like *it's weird that I want a relationship*? This is you fixing that."

But for how long? Roman bit his lip as all his doubts flooded back in. *He's right, it's a pattern. Hell, even Oscar knows that. When does this all go wrong? Any time now.* "I hope so."

"You hope you're happy? Or you're freaking out because you're finally dating a guy you *can* be happy with?"

Roman blinked and stared at Blane. "Uh. That second one?"

"What's the problem, in a sentence?"

That made Roman rub his neck as he tried to cut to the heart of it. "I don't know if I can do this."

"Do what?" Blane had his patient voice on.

"A relationship. At all. Like, rearranging my life, being *that guy* going home to make dinner for his boyfriend at night… I feel like all I know is being, well, Mr. Slick. Picking them up. I don't know how to keep them. And that's no way to be a good boyfriend. I see the way you and Falcon treat each other, or Deen and Nico. Am I really gonna be good enough for him?"

As the last sentence came out, Roman winced. He hadn't meant to say *that* much. Now he just sounded like an insecure loser.

But Blane was patient. "It's a skill. You got good at picking up guys, you can get good at keeping this one around. This is how people change—when they really want to. It can be an internal or external thing, but it's strongest when it's both. Like now, you want to be better at these things for you, but also for him."

Roman nodded slowly. He wasn't convinced, but he was willing to believe it. "If he sticks around that long and I don't scare him off like the rest of them."

"So far he is. He's still living with you, for God's sake," Blane laughed. "And we gave him several outs."

"Good point," Roman admitted.

"Why were you always chasing them off with those long-term dreams?"

Roman had to think about this one. The easy answer was *because that's what I thought I wanted,* and then the slightly harder one came to him: *because it* is *what I want.* Then, like a ton of bricks, "Oh. Because I... I don't know how to bridge the gap. Between here and the future. I'd start dating someone and then fly away for a few weeks." He winced. "That doesn't look good."

"And you're trying to change your schedule to be around him more. That's change." Blane punched his shoulder. "So cheer up and don't let yourself fall into old patterns. Now, what's this about the job?"

"Are you my fairy godmother today?"

"Yeah, but I look better in a dress. And my wand doesn't sparkle... usually. Spill," Blane ordered.

"More than I wanted to know," Roman laughed. "Uh, there's been a thing going on for a while with this guy who's an asshole at work. It finally blew up, and I'm figuring out if I should call HR."

"Duh," Blane snorted. "Why not?"

"The flight deck is one of those boys' clubs." Roman shook his head. "I wasn't running to tell on him."

"Yeah, but the playground isn't a workplace. They can be fucking professionals or get out. And your company's pretty good with human rights, right? They won't fire you for being gay and causing trouble or whatever bullshit reason. They *can* in Tennessee, but yours won't."

"No, they won't," Roman agreed, feeling a surge of gratitude that he was at a huge American airline and not a mom-and-pop freight operation or something. It could be a lot worse. "They'll probably just shuffle him somewhere else. But I don't feel good getting him fired."

"Man." Blane shook his head. "If I had a coworker at the zoo who did the stuff to me that he's done, what would you say?"

Roman was silent for a moment, conceding the point. "Call them."

"What, now?" They were just pulling up to his house, and the suggestion startled him.

"Yeah, now." Blane put the parking brake on and leaned back. "We don't let each other take crap, remember?"

Roman offered a faint smile, too nervous to say anything back as he took his phone out to call the boss—his chief pilot, rather than one of the managers. Mark was strict but fair, and his gut instinct told him Mark would have his back.

"Hey, Mark," he greeted when he picked up. "Uh, do you have a minute?"

"Roman. Hi. Sure. What's up, man?"

Roman found himself looking at Blane, who nodded encouragement. "Uh. Um," Roman stuttered for a moment. "I got a problem and I wasn't sure who to call."

One perk of the industry—nobody lost their head at the first sign of trouble. Mark sounded perfectly calm as he answered, "Okay. Walk me through it."

"Basically," Roman blew out a sigh, his nerves settling as his brain engaged its training. Just the facts. "Cory's been a real pain in my ass since I started. He started saying little things here and there, but it was just banter, you know? Then it got worse, and finally he blew up during our outbound. In Singapore, he picked a public fight in front of the crew while we were at the bar. The flight back was… if not for Ken, man, things could have gotten ugly."

Mark blew out a sigh. "I wondered how long it'd take. I knew he was a jerk sometimes, but not that bad. Jesus. You're right to report it."

"I guess. I just want to stop it happening at work, at least.

I can be professional for eight hours in a cockpit if I need to be. But I *am* transferring back anyway, I think."

"He'll just find someone else to pick on that way. Don't let him drive you away."

"Because I want more time with my boyfriend," Roman said, clear and strong. He was in a free country, goddamn it, and he wasn't going to be ashamed of it. "I'm not running away from him."

"Oh. This is… homophobic stuff from Cory, I take it?"

"Yeah."

"This can become a he-said, he-said mess, but if your crew will you back you up…"

"Oh, yeah. They encouraged me to report it," Roman said. "What's next?"

"I have to talk to people and figure out how HR wants to proceed. They'll probably want to talk to everyone. I'll let you know when I hear back, okay?" Mark told him. "Thanks for calling me."

Roman blinked, the knot in his chest loosening. "Thanks," he answered. "Talk to you later."

As he hung up, he shook his head and looked at Blane. He almost felt hopeful, but he didn't dare hope for any comeuppance. If they talked to him and got him to knock that crap off at work, and if he got a short-haul position again where he didn't have to work with Cory, he'd be happy.

"Good?" Blane prompted.

"Better," Roman admitted. "Thanks, man." He wasn't sure he would have done that unprompted. At least, it might have taken him a few more weeks.

Then, Derek popped into his mind and he realized that wasn't true. It had only started bothering him now that he'd seen Cory's potential abuse of power.

"Good."

"You? Ready to pop the question?" Roman teased.

Blane groaned, but he was smiling. "Yeah, I guess."

"You talked the talk to me. Walk the walk," Roman told him. "Thanks for the ride, man."

Blane mock-saluted, then leaned in to hug him. "Go on, get some sleep. I think someone's waiting for you."

When Roman looked over, the front curtains were moving like they'd just been dropped. He grinned and glanced back at Blane, his heart light with anticipation. "Yeah. See you. Tell me when he says yes and posts Instagram stories about it and all that sappy crap."

"Will do," Blane laughed.

Roman grinned as he clambered out of the car, rolling his bag behind him as he headed for his front door. He was a minute away from having Oscar in his arms again, so everything was right. How could it be anything else?

CHAPTER
Twenty~Five

OSCAR

"THIS IS THE PLACE!"

Even though he'd slept a full night and seemed to be back on Tennessee time, Roman looked dazed as his gaze followed Oscar's gestures.

The studio was shabby right now—it needed some interior work, and Oscar had put off thinking about exactly what that would entail.

"The apartment's at the back," Oscar added and strode over to the longest wall. "Obviously this is where I'll put the mirrors. The floor will be the biggest cost, but the guy from the small business development center is willing to work with me."

"The… papers are signed?"

"Yep." Oscar was still limping and feeling constricted by his brace, but at least he was walking on his own again. The brief rest period had done wonders to get him through that stage of healing. He couldn't push it, so they were heading straight home again after this, but being able to move—even a little—lifted Oscar's spirits. "Scary, huh?"

"I'll say," Roman agreed.

Oscar gradually grew aware that Roman hadn't said much about this place or the deal at all. "So, uh, what do you think?"

"Of the place?" Roman looked around as if assessing it.

"Of everything."

Roman blinked at him. "Um. That's a… broad question."

"It's a broad situation," Oscar teased, wrapping an arm around Roman. He hadn't realized how much he'd grown used to leaning on Roman, despite his initial bruised pride. Even now, he found himself kind of *liking* it.

Especially when Roman's arm slid around his shoulders and pulled him against his chest. Oscar hummed with contentment as Roman's arm stayed around him.

"I guess… I just don't know what's gonna happen now. I've gotten kind of used to this," Roman admitted.

Oscar nodded slightly. "But I need to be independent, too." He couldn't make Roman do all the work here—support him, house him, hell, feed him sometimes. Not only did it rub him wrong because of who he was, but it didn't seem like relationship material.

"I get that." Roman sounded glum, though. "So, the apartment?"

"Oh, it needs some work before it's livable," Oscar shook his head. "It's only a little studio. I'm gonna come here tomorrow and make a list of everything I need to do."

"Okay." Roman squeezed his shoulders. "I'm glad you're gonna do something you want to do. That has to feel good." His tone sounded forced, but Oscar wasn't about to question the sudden change of heart.

"It's cool. It's really… good." Oscar's words failed him and he laughed sheepishly. "I just felt so useless."

"You're not," Roman said immediately and fiercely. "Stop that."

"We've been through this before, haven't we?" Oscar chuckled.

Roman grunted and let him go, then wandered around the place, his eyes everywhere but Oscar's face. "I like it. I can see the potential," he said.

"Just like me," Oscar chuckled under his breath. He gestured around. "Someday, the light will touch all this, and it will be mine. Or something."

Roman laughed. "Yeah, it could use the newspaper off those windows. That'll help."

"Will it ever." Oscar couldn't wait for some more physical work. As long as he didn't push that knee, he could put his upper body to work renovating. Plus, there were a thousand minor details suddenly on his mind: he had to figure out a class schedule, advertise himself, find students and start running classes. The deposit on this place had drained a good chunk of his savings. He could only float a few months' mortgage payments without bringing anything in. Roman touched his shoulder, bringing him out of it. "Huh?"

"I said," Roman chuckled, "you look like you could use a neck rub. Come on, let's get home."

"Sorry. I'm gonna be a basket case for a while," Oscar told Roman with a quick grin.

Roman shrugged. "Me, too. It happens. I think it's part of being an adult."

"Yeah. I guess so," Oscar admitted. He sidled closer to Roman until he could lean into him again. "Okay, I'm sick of bank meetings and lawyer meetings and paperwork out the ass. Let's just go cuddle. If we hurry, we can make it home to a HGTV marathon and yell at the assholes looking for a half-a-million house with a hundred fifty."

"Sounds perfect." Roman sounded distracted again, but he took Oscar's hand and walked at his pace as they made their slow way out to the car.

Something had been off since he'd gotten back last night. As they'd fetched Roman's car, as Roman had given him the sweetest gift of ridiculous salt and pepper shakers from abroad to apologize for leaving so suddenly, something had still been hanging in the air between them.

Oscar swallowed hard, nervous for the first time in a while at the prospect of cuddling with Roman, only silence to fill the space between them.

But he's still here for me.

The first couple minutes of leaning into Roman made Oscar's stress drop from a seven to four. He didn't even realize he was leaning his head on Roman's shoulder until Roman nudged him away enough to kiss him.

"What's up?" Oscar finally asked after a few minutes of the dreaded silence. It was difficult to handle while knowing there were still things up in the air between them. Seeing Roman stare into space and not knowing what was behind those beautiful eyes made him uncomfortable as hell.

"Huh?"

"Something's bothering you. Is this a good time to talk?" Oscar pressed. "I think we're supposed to do that."

Roman winced. "Oh. Yeah. Sorry." He cleared his throat, loosely draping his arm over Oscar's shoulders. "There's just a lot to think about, what with your new studio and my job and stuff."

Oscar could feel him trying to deflect. He kicked Roman's ankle gently. "Try again."

"Like an old married couple already," Roman grumbled teasingly. "I mean, you're... moving out?"

"Well, I have to fix up the apartment first," Oscar said slowly. *Maybe I shouldn't have done this so fast. God, he's basically been away this whole time. But it's not his say what I do...* "Why?"

"I dunno. I just... want to do what makes you happy. But... if it's anything I did..."

"Oh, fuck." Oscar hadn't realized until now how Roman might take it, what with his habit of overcommitment. "No, hon. It's just... we should date like regular people, right? Come over and see each other sometimes, go out to eat, you know. That stuff. And then there's Christmas. I should be moved out in time for that."

Roman looked skeptical. "I guess. Do you want to?"

"I guess. Do you?"

Roman shrugged and nodded. "It sounds... okay..."

He doesn't want me around? Oscar's brow furrowed, and he rubbed his forehead. The exhaustion from the whole damn process of buying his first property had set in, making it hard to think straight.

It wasn't aided by his own anxiety. The more he thought about it, the more worrying it was that they were already having this much trouble talking. They'd gotten too close too fast, and the idea that he could fuck up the relationship that way was scary.

Oscar had never had something like this, and he didn't want to lose it. Or, he realized, he didn't want to be the last to know when it was already lost. He'd always been the first to leave.

And nobody ever wants me to stay. Not really.

Oscar rose to his feet. "I think I'm gonna go pick up supplies so I can start tomorrow before the stores open." Might as well put his goddamn dawn rising habit to use. And get out of here before he cried all over Roman like a clingy boyfriend.

"Okay." Roman looked confused, but his acceptance somehow irritated Oscar even more.

"Okay."

Oscar was halfway to the door when Roman's phone went off. Despite the annoyance and frustration and anxiety churning away in his stomach, he couldn't help but listen in to Roman's end of the conversation.

"Yes, it's Roman. Sorry, when? Today? Uh…" Roman looked up at the wall clock. "Yeah, I can make it. Okay. Thanks."

"Work?" Oscar didn't mean it to sound as catty as it did.

Roman flinched. "Sort of, yeah. HR meeting."

Oscar paused, his jacket halfway on. "What?"

"It's nothing. I'll explain later. I gotta go if I'm gonna—no, I'll change first. Have fun at the hardware store, babe." Roman headed for the master bedroom at a brisk stride.

Oscar stared after Roman, then looked at the door. "Need me to come along?" he called out after a moment of indecision. The distance between them had never been present before, and he didn't know what to do about it.

"No, it'll just be boring waiting around," Roman answered. "Go have fun pottering around the new place. Don't forget we're meeting the guys tonight."

Right… it was Friday again. Oscar's days had been filled with enforced rest or frenetic meetings, and no in-between.

How they were gonna explain all of this if anyone asked, he didn't know. He welled up but rubbed his eyes with frustration. If Roman had some work thing going on, that would explain everything. Now wasn't the time to push his issues onto him again.

"Good luck. See you later," he managed without his voice cracking, then slipped outside.

I'm a shitty boyfriend anyway, he thought as he headed for the car, rubbing the wetness from his eyes with his thumbs. *If this is the beginning of the end, it's probably better for us both.*

"Hey." The young man who ran up to Roman as he grabbed the car door handle looked vaguely familiar in a passing way, and strikingly handsome.

Having dated a dancer for a month, Roman instantly recognized his build and lifted his chin in greeting. "Hi."

"Is Oscar home?"

Instantly, Roman felt suspicious. He hadn't seen anyone coming over to talk to him before now. It could be something to do with the sale, but he hadn't heard much of Oscar's work life. "No, you just missed him."

The man's eyes flashed with annoyance and Roman instantly took a disliking to him. There was something about the way he held himself—not graceful, like Oscar, but self-important. "Well, where is he?" he demanded.

Roman raised a brow to remind him of his manners, but when he didn't even seem to notice, he asked, "And who are you?"

"A dancer," the man said impatiently, as if he were too slow to notice that.

That sealed Roman's decision—no way was he letting Oscar know the guy was around. "I'll let him know someone's looking for him. I have to be somewhere now," he told the guy and pulled open his car door.

"Fine. Don't be a jealous bitch," the man muttered under his breath as he turned on his heel and strode off.

That was interesting. Roman hadn't asked many questions about Oscar's circle of friends, and now he was glad. But if, as he generally found, the statement was more revealing of the person who said it, there were jealous exes on the scene. Oscar had never even let on. Roman's concern grew another notch or two.

He pulled his phone out and sent a quick text before he drove: *Some pretty dancer with a bad temper who wouldn't say who he was demanded to know where you were. I didn't say. Let me know if you need someone to snap him and I'll be there ASAP. He looks twiggier than you.*

Then he turned his phone to vibrate and pocketed it after glancing at the response: *LOL. I'm fine, just ignore him. Thanks for the heads up.*

"Okay. Meeting," he told himself, swallowing back the nervousness. One thing at a time: he shut off his anxiety and drove.

Walking into the office of their corporate headquarters and seeing Cory sitting in the chair opposite the HR manager's desk drove it home: this was serious.

Roman's gut lurched. He nodded once at Cory, who didn't acknowledge him, then dropped into the chair. He refused to scoot it further away from the other man, even if their shoulders were almost touching because of his sheer size.

"Roman. Thank you for coming." Mark was on the other side of the desk, and Loretta, who had led him into the office, joined him there. He rose to his feet to shake hands, and Roman did the same.

"Now that we're all here," Loretta said briskly, "I've discussed the allegations with Mark and with Cory already. Roman, this mediation session isn't designed to take sides. Can you just describe in the simplest facts what happened?"

Roman caught Mark rolling his eyes slightly and almost smiled. Pilots felt that most people didn't know how to handle pilots. He was perfectly relaxed right now, as if he were sitting behind the controls and in charge of hundreds of people's lives. That state of mind wasn't conducive to exaggeration.

"It started with small comments about *my* kind of people. I didn't really care about that. Then he started making jibes about how, like, it must be easier for me to pick up guys in other countries than it is for him to find girls. Implying that my dating choices are because of my sexual orientation, and that they're weird. A lot of needling."

Loretta was taking notes, nodding now and then.

"I thought he was mending bridges once and took him to a bar when he asked, and things got much worse from there on. He used everything he witnessed in little conversations. I finally told him it was unprofessional, and things… came to a head while we were on the clock one day." He glanced at Cory.

Cory was staring ahead at nothing in particular, his jaw set.

Roman rubbed his hand down his face, annoyed that he

hadn't had a chance to shave that morning. He felt scruffy. "He made inappropriate comments that I won't repeat, and I told him that enough was enough, and he wouldn't say that stuff to me while we're at work. It seemed fine until he came up to a group of us at the bar in Singapore a few days ago and implied that I'd get hung for being gay in Singapore."

They could have heard a pin drop.

"The exact words were," Roman used his pilot's sense of recall to pull the exact phrase from his mind, "*Just came to see what's hanging. Apparently, Roman. Or he could be.*"

Mark sucked in his breath and looked over at Cory.

Cory still said nothing, folding his arms and staring through the wall behind the other two.

"We asked him to clarify it and he said it was just a joke again, then stumbled off." Roman glanced between them. "I can clarify the exact comments, but I think that one alone says enough."

"Thank you, Roman. Cory," Loretta began.

He cut her off. "I don't know if that's what I said. I was drunk."

"Perhaps you can clarify what you allegedly said in the cockpit, then."

"Nope. Can't remember that."

"I hope you weren't drunk then," Mark cut in, his tone flat. He'd picked a side, then.

Cory looked at him flatly and shook his head. "Obviously not. But I don't keep track of every little joke I make with a *friend*," he emphasized. "Or someone I thought of as one."

Roman drew a deep breath and sighed. "Do you really want me to say what you said, man? Don't make me do it."

He was really fucking reluctant to out anyone—ever—however much of a dick they were being. Plus, if he said what Cory had told him, it turned this into a sexual harassment liability, and Cory's job was definitely fucked.

"Go ahead," Cory told him. "I bet it won't shake out the way you think."

"Gentlemen," Loretta interjected. "If Cory doesn't remember saying anything that could be misconstrued, perhaps you can clarify for us," she nodded at Roman.

Roman gave a small, tight smile. He looked down for a few moments, his hands twisting together.

But everyone was right—Ken and the crew, Blane... and Oscar would be pissed if he knew. He was going to have to explain this, and he wasn't going to tell Oscar he'd backed down now.

The awful possibility that Cory had said or done worse to someone without Roman's rank or seniority crept into the back of his mind again, and the decision was made. "If he'd just said it off the clock, it wouldn't be as big a deal to me," he said slowly. "But we were in the cockpit—alone—and he... made an indecent proposal that I definitely never invited. Just out of the blue. I told him not to do that ever again." Roman's cheeks flushed as he glanced between the other two, avoiding looking at Cory.

Cory sucked his breath in, and Roman could tell from his peripheral vision that he was glaring at him. "I never wanted you to *do it*. I wanted to make sure you wouldn't."

Roman blinked a few times and finally looked at him. "What?"

"Are you saying you said that?" Loretta interjected.

"No. Yeah. I don't know," Cory snapped, but his gaze was on Roman. "But I didn't want you getting in my pants."

"*Didn't?*" Roman questioned, his brows so high his forehead hurt. "Inviting me to—issuing the invitation you did was a *test*? All those months of baiting me for being gay? Is this because you didn't want me treating you like you say you treat girls? Not that I've ever seen evidence of that," he couldn't resist interjecting. *Have I ever seen him actually with these supposed girlfriends? What if it's all made up and he's so deep in the closet he's buried under his winter parkas?*

Loretta sharply called attention to herself by tapping the desk. "Gentlemen," she said again. "Let's not devolve to a shouting match here."

"Fine. I said things. Whatever," Cory waved a hand. "I didn't want to be left alone with that guy. Look at the size of him. And he's into guys? I don't think that's appropriate…"

Roman tuned him out, but kept storing up his words in the back of his mind while he shoved his emotions back into the boxes from which they were threatening to burst free. Cory was saying something about *if this were a woman* and *lawsuit potential.*

"I think I've heard enough," Mark cut in. "Are you alleging that Roman has ever said or done anything inappropriate towards you?"

Roman looked over at Cory, whose cheeks were spotty red with anger. Huh. He hadn't seen *that* before. "No," Cory spat out. "But he could have. It's a risk."

"Roman, if you could give us some privacy—actually, feel free to head home," Mark said, glancing at Loretta. "We may need to talk to you again, and if you decide you want to press charges…"

"No," Roman said quickly. "No, that's fine. I just want the, pardon my French, crazy shit to stop in the cabin. I don't care if he hates me outside that. I do care if he tries to turn me in to the authorities somewhere it's illegal to be gay, and I do care if he brings all that into our workplace when we have our jobs to be doing. Now that I've applied to transfer, if he's still on long-hauls, it's not a problem for *me*, but I doubt I'm the only gay guy on deck."

He barely remembered being seen out to his car, only snapping back to when he was behind the wheel of his car.

It's not going to go well for him, is it? Roman rubbed his face, trying not to replay the ugly details of that meeting. As much as he tried to resist driving on autopilot, with such intimate knowledge of how wrong it could go, he barely noticed the drive home until he was walking in the front door of his quiet, empty house.

His heart sank. "Oscar?" he tried.

Gone again.

With the timing of him running into that snobby asshole in the driveway, Roman couldn't help a twinge of worry for him. He dug out his phone, but before he texted, he winced. Would it sound too… well, jealous?

Roman dropped onto the couch without even taking his shoes off, his breath whooshing out.

His real problem wasn't with that guy. For all he knew, one of Oscar's friends had an attitude problem. They *were* dancers, after all. Hell, pilots had worse attitudes.

It was too late to go back on his transfer request. Switching back and forth more than once in a year would just look bad. But coming home to an empty house every night…

"Oh, God," he muttered under his breath and buried his face in his hands. What if he lost Oscar *and* his slick lifestyle?

No, he needed him with an intensity he'd been missing for years. Casually picking guys up was fun, but it wasn't lying awake at night with an ache in his chest because he missed skin contact with Oscar so much. It wasn't grinning like a loon when he walked into the house and Oscar had supper and a warm bed ready for him to recover from a long flight. It wasn't dropping Oscar's name into conversations as little as possible and still doing it too often.

That was it. He was going to the studio, and along the way, he was picking up a few things. It was either going to fuck things up with Oscar or make everything right again, but this weird silence couldn't continue.

Roman had to come clean about everything, including what he wanted: Oscar in his house and bed, every day, forever. He couldn't let himself dwell on the possibility it might not work.

This was his best chance, so for once in his life, he was going to let himself be impulsive and follow his heart. It had led him to Oscar in the first place—it couldn't be wrong now.

CHAPTER
Twenty-Seven
OSCAR

"OH, GOD. WHAT HAVE I DONE?"

Without the rose-tinted glasses of taking the first look at his new living and working space, and without a friendly shoulder at his side, Oscar hadn't expected everything to crash into him at once.

He couldn't untangle the knot of emotions that flooded him: fear, anticipation, frustration, nostalgia, and a certain sadness, too.

Oscar dropped his bucket of cleaning supplies by the door: mop, broom, window cleaner, and cloths. Everything he'd brought was going to see heavy use today.

The place was dirty—it had sat unused for a few months before going on the market, and then hadn't sold for a few more. Dust had added to dust. How the hell could that much dust accumulate so fast?

He could see why the place hadn't sold; the renovations were enough to put anyone off, and there were several yoga and dance studios already in the area. Pole was all the rage now, and the turf was thoroughly claimed by two pole studios.

And the studio apartment at the back. Oh, fuck. There was no way it was livable—the bathroom was moldy in corners, the kitchen was missing most of its appliances and cabinet doors, the bedrooms smelled funky, and one window needed repairs.

No wonder the seller had given him a break for coming in under list price "in respect of the renovations that were necessary," as his realtor had put it. The surveyor had agreed. All those little flags Oscar had ignored, because it was in his price range and it *felt* like the right move to make.

But how much of that had been trying to run from his feelings of… what was it? Being a burden on others? Roman, in particular? His need to find something to keep himself busy? Well, this fit the bill. Even if he focused on the dance studio, he wasn't a DIY expert. It would take at least two weeks to get into shape to actually start teaching classes.

And that was deliberately ignoring all the work to be done on the apartment. He could really only do one thing at once. Oscar's brain skittered back and forth between the halves of the building, and the overwhelm threatened to choke him.

His phone buzzed, and his heart leapt. *Roman?* He'd gotten a text from him while he was at the hardware store about that asshole sniffing around—which had to be Jef—but Roman hadn't texted again since then.

Oscar had spent a good half-hour feeling bad about not going with Roman, whatever Roman said. After all, *he'd* tried to turn down company before the meeting at which he'd been fired. Roman hadn't listened. Maybe he should be better at not listening, too.

He had to squash the hope before it even had time to take root—the notification was a text message from Matt.

Xmas lunch in town. Last day before we hit the road! Get your ass over here.

It would look petty not to go, Oscar knew that. But he wasn't sure he could handle seeing everyone hyped up with pre-tour jitters, half-focused on their own notes from the final rehearsals.

On the other hand, staying here didn't sound like all that much fun when the newspaper-covered windows and dingy walls were closing in around him. He couldn't stop fucking wasting his time thinking about Roman letting him move out. That wasn't helping him do what he needed to do to get this place livable.

What did he have to lose?

On my way, he answered and spitefully nudged his bucket away from the door with his toe. "I'll get around to it," he said sullenly, answering the critic in his own head. "It's only Christmas once."

The weight in Oscar's chest didn't lift as he said it, and he tried not to feel like he was running away from his chance at a new life before he'd even gotten started.

It was just one lunch. *Then* he could deal with the future.

***

"Look what the cat dragged in."

The uncomfortable laughter that followed Jef's comment was subdued in an instant when Oscar turned his glare on them.

What the hell had happened in a few short weeks to the guys who had told him to knock it off?

"Matt's allowed to say that," Oscar told Jef, unafraid to meet his look. "You're not."

"Oh, excuse me, princess. Am I allowed to say hello?"

"No." Oscar let his attention turn to the other dancers as he took the chair Matt had saved for him. It looked like everyone had eaten already, so he didn't bother asking for a menu himself. "What's been up, then? Final rehearsals going well?"

There were another few moments of uncomfortable silence. *Okay, what the hell?* Oscar looked around to catch Raj's eye, but he wasn't there. It was beginning to feel like he was outnumbered, and he didn't like that feeling. He didn't have a problem with anyone here but Jef, after all.

"Not bad, yeah," Matt answered finally, looking weirdly embarrassed.

"Those of us with major roles," said Alexei, with whom Oscar had never gotten along well, "have been hard at work for these weeks." His English was less heavily accented than it had been when he'd first joined the company, but it was still sharp in the silence.

"Right. Yeah, that's what I said," Oscar said slowly, then glanced at Matt. Was he relegated to some background role?

Matt wouldn't meet his gaze.

Finally, Gregory huffed a sigh. "Jesus. Don't let this spoil the Christmas mood, guys."

"Not my fault," Jef spoke up from the end of the table. Someone reached out to touch his arm and someone else started talking to him quietly. Again, though, it felt less like defusing than people choosing sides.

Oscar gritted his jaw and looked over at Matt when conversation finally resumed slowly. "So you're background scenery?"

"Pretty much," Matt mumbled. "I might have gotten into an… argument."

"Oh, Jesus. Not over me?" Matt's silence confirmed it, and Oscar squeezed his arm. "Hon. No, your career comes first. Mine's tanked. Don't take yours down." The guys around him—most of them, anyway—tried to disagree, but Oscar wouldn't let them. "It's not me being overly dramatic this time. It's true. So I'm picking up teaching. I got the mortgage on a studio."

The phrases "skulking around" and "poaching" were distinctly audible from the other end of the table.

Oscar snorted, unable to resist taking the bait. "My students' ages and skill levels wouldn't remotely be poaching from our—you guys. Or are you just worried about competition?" He smiled sweetly at Jef. "Speaking of skulking around, what were you doing talking to my boyfriend?"

Jef looked like he was considering arguing that it hadn't been him.

Oscar raised a brow. "Don't even try that. Be honest, for once in your life."

"Well, I don't know about you, but I'm done with this conversation," Jef announced and rose to his feet. "Those of you I've pre-selected, please accompany me to the studio for one more debrief."

It was a slap in the face: a reminder that Jef had all the power in the world over the company, and he intended to use it to undermine any friendships Oscar had left.

But Matt stood up, too. "No. I need to rest, and I'm going to do it while I catch up with an old friend."

A few others nodded, but over half of the dancers started shifting, slowly rising to their feet with guilty expressions and gathering their thick winter coats. Getting dressed against the cold gave them an excuse not to look at Oscar.

Jef flagged down the waiter and gestured toward his end of the table. "All these checks as one, please."

It became painfully obvious what was going on. Sure, principal dancers were responsible for setting the mood and building a sense of unity among the company, but this was beyond the pale.

"If you want to stay and damage your career prospects—" Jef started.

Matt just smiled. "You don't have any power over me. You know why? I'm done. After this show, I'm out."

Oscar choked on air for a second. Matt hadn't had the same career trajectory as him, but he still had a good five to ten years left. What the fuck was he doing? He hissed and tugged Matt's sleeve.

"It's not just about Oscar. I made my mind up a long time ago," Matt told him. "If people decided to be morons higher up and didn't see what you're doing to this company... if they let you sneak up the ranks—pay or fuck your way up, I don't care how you did it—I'd leave and find my own way somewhere else. You've got talent, but not enough to rest that ego on. It's going to topple the whole damn tower. I don't blame all of you sticking by him. It's smart," he said, glancing down at Oscar. "Which is why this idiot is trying to tear my sleeve off," he added. He affectionately ruffled Oscar's hair to get him to let go.

It worked, and Oscar scowled at Matt as he patted his hair back into place. "You're an idiot, too, but at least I can respect that."

Jef glared at Matt. "Fine. Don't be surprised to see your-self out of work."

"Is that a threat?"

"Statement," Jef said with a smooth smile.

Oscar cleared his throat. "Well, I'm going to need help at the new studio. I'd rather have a friendly face than someone who will use me until he gets a big break and then stab me in the back with a snake-oil smile."

The waiter was frozen, lingering near Jef with the check in one hand and credit card machine in the other. The restaurant was quiet, other diners listening in.

"Oh, fuck you." Jef's composure finally snapped. He dug his wallet out. "I hope your pathetic little studio dies. No, worse: you get stuck teaching bratty ten-year-olds how to one-two-step at the county fair." Jef shoved cash into the waiter's hand and pushed past him, his expression tight. "I was *trying* to warn Oscar to go quietly to pasture, but it looks like I'll have to fight him."

"Like he can do a thing. He never did respect teachers," Matt observed idly, his hand on Oscar's shoulder.

Oscar resisted the urge to get the last word in. The anxiety and fear that had knotted his chest when he'd unlocked the studio earlier were gone now, replaced by the intense drive—the *need*, really—that had fueled his career until he'd lost it. He'd thought he'd never feel that again.

"Thanks." Oscar cleared his throat and glanced around at the handful of guys who had stayed, too—all at Matt's end of the table. There had obviously already been a division he hadn't spotted. "And you guys, too."

"Don't mention it. I just wasn't done my salad," Jon said with a wink.

"I think I'm gonna take off in a minute, actually," Oscar admitted, sinking into his chair. "I just picked up the keys, and…Jesus. The place is a mess."

"Well…" Matt cast a crafty look around the table. "If you need some helping hands…"

"Oh, God. I can't ask you guys to help, man." Oscar knew what kind of shape their bodies were in after intensive rehearsals, and nightly performances ahead.

"No, but we can offer," Matt told him. "Give us cloths or something. Let us polish something."

"There you go, trying to polish my metal again," Oscar joked to hide the tears he was blinking out of his eyes. "If you *must*."

"I'll come too," Andy offered, and then Jon nodded. One by one, all the guys still sitting at the table joined in to say they'd help.

Oscar wiped his cheeks roughly and cleared his throat. "Right. Let me, uh, call a couple Ubers for you or whatever."

He strode outside to do it so he could recover his composure, zipping up his jacket against the cold but smiling so hard it hurt.

Maybe it would feel like old times, just for a moment. And maybe that would be long enough.

CHAPTER
Twenty-Eight
ROMAN

IT WAS DO OR DIE TIME. ROMAN'S HEART POUNDED AS HE strode down the sidewalk to the storefront covered in yellowing newspaper, his best chance at making up tucked under his arm.

He nearly missed the storefront and had to back up a few paces. It didn't look anything like it had before. The newspaper had been torn down, and there were half a dozen guys on the other side of the window, buffing the inside with cloths.

Roman stopped on the spot, blinking. Then one of the guys spotted the flowers poking out of the bucket under his arm and Roman heard a faint "aww," followed by all of them —Oscar included—turning to look at him.

Well, there went his element of surprise.

Roman's cheeks flushed as he stepped up to the door, and Oscar pulled it open before he could even knock. "Uh. Hi. Sorry, I didn't know there was a party…"

Oscar waved it off, relief written all over his face. "You made it out of the meeting."

"Yeah. Yeah, I'll tell you about that later," Roman promised, clearing his throat and fishing the bouquet out. "I wanted to, uh, say sorry for being so weird about everything, and ask you to live with me, because—oh, shit, that wasn't in the right order. I mean, the bouquet is like, you know how people give dancers bouquets on opening nights? Of course you know."

The guys—all dancers, by the looks of them—were clearly trying to hold in laughter, some more successfully than others.

Even Oscar was biting his lower lip, holding back laughter.

Roman, even more flustered, cleared his throat and thrust the bouquet at his boyfriend. "Will you keep living with me? I like coming home to you, and I don't want you moving somewhere you'll probably fall through a hole in the floor and put out your other knee. Shit, that was less than sensitive."

Oscar was laughing richly now, that warm sound echoing around the empty place. "I love you, you great big loony." He looped his arms around Roman's shoulders and squeezed hard enough that Roman couldn't breathe for a moment.

Roman couldn't squeeze Oscar that hard in return lest he snap him, but he squished him as tightly as he felt comfortable doing, one-armed. He was still holding the bucket and feeling kind of dumb now.

"And what's that?" Oscar asked, pointing at the bucket.

Roman lifted it up so he couldn't look inside. "First you gotta tell me if you're moving out. And if so, if you want to keep being with me."

Oscar looked sheepish. "I just assumed you wanted me out of your hair. You... really want me to stay?"

"Duh," Roman snorted, and Oscar laughed. "I love you, too. I have no idea what the fuck I'm doing in a relationship or how to, like, tell you what I'm feeling, but I'm working on it. Maybe I'll even get the words in the right order sometime."

Oscar smiled gently. "Then yeah, I wanna keep living with you. Not just because there's a hole in the floor in that apartment. There's no appliances. And the bathroom door won't close."

Roman's eyes widened. "Jesus. How bad am I if you were considering that?"

"Not that bad," Oscar laughed. "It's not weird we only just started to date, though?"

"It's a little weird we're saying all of this in front of your friends," Roman pointed out, unable to resist a smirk. "But I'm fine with keeping going how we are right now."

Oscar's cheeks flushed and he jolted like he'd forgotten they were there. He set the flowers down against the window. "Oh, shit. Right. Uh, guys, Roman. My boyfriend."

One of them, who was staring as if enchanted, covering his mouth with his left hand and sporting an engagement ring, finally lowered his hand. "Yeah, I guessed. Where the hell were you hiding *this* guy? I'm Matt."

They introduced themselves in a rush, hurrying over to shake hands and clap Oscar's back.

"Oooh. Champagne." It was Matt again, who had also pointed out Roman's presence outside, peeking in the bucket.

"Jesus, you're taking all my thunder today," Roman complained with a laugh.

Matt laughed. "Oops. Sorry. But I'd say you have a little thunder left for your boyfriend," he gave Roman an up-and-down look and winked. "Especially now that we've got the place cleaned up. We'll just… head out now."

"Oh, fuck off, you perv," Oscar told him and cuffed him upside the head.

Roman tried to pretend that hadn't just given him ideas. There was bound to be a spot out of sight of those windows here, right?

"Anyway, let me show you the apartment," Oscar added after a moment. "No holes, I promise. In the floor."

Roman laughed as hard as the rest of them as Oscar sashayed off to the door at the back of the place.

"Good luck with that one," Matt added, playfully sticking his tongue out. "But no, dude, really. We're leaving early. We gotta split," he called out to Oscar, who rushed back for a round of hugs. Roman tried to stay out of the way but found himself the victim of a few hugs and Christmas greetings anyway.

Once they were gone in a whirlwind like—well, like a *dance*—the energy seemed to linger here anyway. It was happier here.

Or maybe that was just him.

"Did they really leave us alone here to have sex?"

"I think so," Oscar grinned. "Now, what's in the bucket?"

Roman handed it over and laughed. "Window cleaner and champagne. I was gonna, like, do the windows for you to say sorry for being dumb and not asking for what I wanted."

Oscar's gaze softened. He set down the bucket and looped his arms around Roman's waist, and Roman slid his arms around Oscar's shoulders to hold him close. "It's not just you," Oscar told him. "I don't know what I'm doing either. We've been over that by now. I just… never thought to ask.

I'm not good at asking for help and letting people… be there for me."

"That's why you have friends—and a boyfriend—to be there for you, and make sure you get help when you need it," Roman said firmly. "Like helping renovate this—and shush, I'm not taking no for an answer. On that leg, you're not doing any heavy construction work, mister." Before Oscar could argue, he smirked and gave him a distraction. "And to give me some awfully good ideas."

"Like what?" Oscar asked, his lips quirking into a playful smile as he gave up on the urge he always seemed to have to resist letting anyone else help him out—for now, at least.

"Such as…" Roman drawled, bending over enough to pick up the bottle, "popping this open, and christening the place."

Oscar giggled, resting his forehead on Roman's shoulder when he straightened up again. "Sounds perfect," he murmured. "Not very romantic, though."

"Anything can be romantic if you're there, too," Roman murmured back, kissing the top of his head. "Is it more romantic if I add a blowjob?"

Oscar laughed louder, pulling back and stretching onto tiptoe to press a firm kiss against Roman's lips. "My self-interest says yes."

"We have time before we leave to see the guys. Show me this place you were planning to hide from me in." Roman winked.

"I wasn't *hiding*," Oscar grumbled, pulling away from Roman as he sashayed back to the door. Roman noticed his gait was much more even now, even though the leg of his jeans still bulged with the shape of the brace underneath. "You're not gonna let that go, are you?"

"I'm not letting *you* go," Roman added firmly, pulling off the cage of the cork and popping the bottle as he followed. "Tell you what, though. I forgot to get plastic cups. We'll have to drink straight from the fountain." He caught Oscar's eye and licked the foam trickling down the side of the bottle.

Oscar's cheeks turned red and he nearly fell over himself in his haste to get the apartment door open.

Roman doubled down one more time, his confidence finally returning. Seeing Oscar so flustered made his heart swell with pride and pleasure. "We kind of skipped all the foreplay in this relationship, didn't we? Well, we've got time now. And access," he raised a brow meaningfully. "That's a perk of living together, if you needed more convincing. But I'm glad you didn't. I almost had to do my speech: you can check out, but you can never leave… my heart. Or something. I hadn't thought that part out, if you *did* want to leave."

Oscar grabbed him and hauled him through the door to close it again, making Roman laugh. "Get your ass in here."

"Someone's got a *load* of attitude all stored up for me," Roman smirked, handing Oscar the bottle and dropping to his knees in the front hallway. Beyond, he saw a glimpse at the apartment, but he had something more interesting in his field of vision.

Oscar squeaked, "You don't even want to… the kitchen… see the place…?"

"There's time later," Roman murmured, pressing his lips against the bulge in Oscar's pants and backing him up against the wall. "Come on, drink up. I sure as hell plan to."

Oscar could barely stop giggling long enough to drink from the bottle. His hand rested on Roman's shoulder, his thumb rubbing in gentle circles that spoke volumes.

And when Roman swallowed Oscar's hardening shaft in one quick motion, Oscar's whimper of delight was music to Roman's ears: the tune that he was now utterly certain could make his heart race and his soul sing forever.

CHAPTER
Twenty~Nine
ROMAN

NOBODY COULD FAIL TO NOTICE OSCAR'S CHEEKS FLUSHING every goddamn time Roman looked at Oscar. So, of course, he was having the time of his life doing it as much as possible.

"Now that the secret's out, the two of you are gross and coupley," Deen finally observed, grinning at them. "All it took was a little interrogation."

"Oh, yeah. About that." Roman put down his beer and glared sternly at the rest of them. "Taking advantage of my boyfriend's, er… slender frame."

"If you're saying I can't handle my drinks," Oscar scolded, sitting bolt upright and folding his arms, "you can fuck off."

"That sounds like drunk talk," Tyler laughed. "What have you been giving that boy?"

"Just half a bottle of champagne."

"And you said *we* were plying him for information!" Dustin exclaimed. "Look at the size of him."

"Fuck off," Oscar informed them, scowling, and they just laughed—Roman included.

It was good to see him getting along so well with the rest of them, much more comfortable than he had seemed before. Apparently all he'd needed was a little light peer pressure.

"Whatever. Don't get my boyfriend drunk. That's my job," Roman insisted, trying to save some grace.

"Well, they're challenging us to predrink next time," Blane told Falcon.

"If *that's* what you're getting from this," Falcon shook his head and rolled his eyes. "It still won't make me do your laundry."

"Are you sure? Even the rosé you really like?"

"I'll drink whatever you give me, but I won't do the laundry. That's your job."

"Ahh, engagement bliss," Dustin murmured loudly enough for everyone to hear.

They laughed and Blane pouted before admitting, "It *is* my job."

"Don't look so sad. You need clean clothes to bring to Paris, unless you plan to buy them there." Before Blane could say it, Falcon laughed and added, "We are *not* bringing three suitcases of new clothes home just because you didn't do laundry."

"Fine, fine."

When Roman glanced over at Dustin, despite his teasing words, there was a strange look on his face as he looked at his hands. Roman caught his breath when he noticed Dustin rubbing his ring finger, so idly he might not even be aware he was doing it.

He nudged Oscar, but by the time Oscar looked over, it was too late.

Is he feeling it now? Roman couldn't blame him—watching Nico and then Blane find love had been strangely difficult, which made more sense now that he'd dropped the playboy act and admitted what he'd really wanted all along.

Dustin spoke up, "Are you going to Paris this weekend?"

"Next," Falcon told them all, beaming ear-to-ear. "We've been planning the itinerary every evening."

"Well, you guys get to skip out, then… but I was thinking we could find a weekend day that works and have a work party at Oscar's new studio."

Oscar yelped, then glared at him. "It's not fair to…"

"Shut up," Nico told him affectionately and clapped him on the shoulder, looking at Roman. "What do you need?"

"Renos. I know a couple of you," here he looked at Josh, "handle tools all day."

"Heh. As often as I can." Josh winked.

"The place needs some fixing up, especially the kitchen. Don't tell him, but if he'll let me, I'm helping pay for some renovations for his Christmas gift."

Oscar was a funny shade of pink now, looking torn between laughter and feeling sentimental. "Oh," he murmured under his breath.

"If we can get the labor for free, it'll be cheap to get it fixed up—at least, good enough to start teaching classes."

The enthusiasm around the table ratcheted up.

"That's awesome," Deen enthused. Of all people, he knew the self-employment struggle perhaps the best. "Of course we'll help. We can take it in shifts if not everyone can make it at the same time."

Oscar's eyes were brimming, and they pretended not to notice. Roman wrapped his arm around his boyfriend's shoulders.

"And there's one other thing. The transfer's official, and,

uh. I think I got a guy fired." The silence that fell made Roman blush with the attention suddenly on him. "Long story short, Blane made me do it," he laughed uncomfortably. "This guy was making jokes that started becoming, you know, more and more pointed. Finally, he tried to hit on me at work."

"At work, as in… in the cockpit? Of a plane? That was in the air?" Falcon yelped. "What the fuck!"

"Yeah." Roman grimaced. "HR is just glad I'm not pressing charges or a lawsuit against anyone. And honestly, I don't think I was his only target. Getting him fired is the only thing I could really do, which is shitty, but…" he trailed off, raising his shoulders in a shrug.

"Harassing people isn't right, ever," Blane said firmly. "I'm proud of you, man. You spoke up for a lot of people who couldn't speak up, I bet."

"Yeah." Josh scowled. "If we couldn't kick his ass, at least you got *some* justice."

"It feels so anticlimactic. We just, like, had some bullshit mediation session and he admitted to everything and then… that was it." Roman shook his head. "But I guess it's more important what I do now. I don't wanna let any of that shit fly under the radar anymore."

Oscar squeezed his arm, his brows furrowed. "Thank you for telling me," he said softly. "Us."

"Yeah. I'll kick your ass if you hide your problems from us again, though," Blane added, and Roman flipped him off.

"Bright side is, I'm pretty much out to everyone," Roman grinned. "And they wanna meet you at the Christmas party."

"Me?" Oscar exclaimed with a quiet laugh. "Why?"

"The guy who made Mr. Slick not so slick," Josh

commented with a grin. "Hell, it took us all aback too. But it's good to see you two being happy and gross."

Roman knew he was blushing just as fiercely as Oscar. "Thanks."

Finally, he wasn't hiding a thing from anyone, and he felt free.

Thirty

OSCAR

"I'VE BEEN WAITING GODDAMN LONG ENOUGH."

The Uber hadn't even pulled away from the curb before Roman expressed his sentiment.

"To be home?" Oscar winked. "With me? Just the two of us, and a house to ourselves?"

Roman kicked his shoes off and threw his jacket in the closet, then stepped into the living room and waited for Oscar to undress. "Oh, yeah. And a whole night to ourselves. One of many to come."

Being watched like prey made Oscar squirm from foot to foot, struggling to get the zipper undone. He finally stepped out of his coat and tossed it aside with a derisive snort. "Stupid thing. I've got better things to be doing."

"In a better place," Roman agreed. He pounced—he picked Oscar up and tossed him over his shoulder.

"Roma—oh my God," Oscar laughed, trying to keep his voice down. The buzz from the champagne had faded, thankfully, or he might not know up from down right now.

At least he had a great view of Roman's ass. "You're a pilot, not a caveman."

"Would you rather I made airplane noises? I could do that." Roman started making *brrr* and *neeeow* noises and Oscar lost it.

He was still laughing so hard he couldn't breathe when Roman tossed him on the bed and shut the door. "I love you," Oscar told him, beaming up at Roman as Roman straddled him and kissed him.

"I love you too," Roman murmured against his lips, brushing their noses together affectionately. "And I'm glad I can say that without worrying about scaring you off now."

"Don't ever worry about that," Oscar told him firmly, his hands resting on Roman's shoulder blades. He rubbed Roman's back lightly. "You haven't managed to yet, and you won't. Not by sharing what you want. Maybe I won't always agree, but at least I'll *know*."

Roman gazed at him, cupping his cheek. "Huh. I didn't think of it that way."

"We could have avoided a bunch of angst by just saying *I don't want you to move out* and *I don't want to move out, but I feel like a burden*," Oscar shrugged, then squirmed with embarrassment as Roman's eyes sharpened. "And if you'd told me what was going on at work, I could have supported you."

"That was my bad," Roman agreed. "But if I can change the subject… you still feel like a burden?"

"Not… exactly. I'm trying to get used to it," Oscar admitted. "It's… okay not to be on my own two feet all the time when I have people like you and Falcon and the brothers around."

Roman pressed gentle kisses to his lips. "That's right. We

love you for you, not because you don't require any energy from us."

Oscar stared for a few moments. "Oh. That's… oh."

"And I'll try to, uh, stop daydreaming so hard about the future that I forget to say what I want," Roman said with a grin. "We'll work this out."

"At least we speak the same language," Oscar murmured with a cheeky smile, deciding to shelve the revelation for a bit later. He had a lot to think about all of a sudden, and all he wanted for now was Roman in his arms.

"What's that?"

"Touch me," Oscar whispered, digging his nails into Roman's back. He licked his lips. "Let me feel your body on mine. Finger me and fuck me until I beg you to let me come."

Roman's cheeks flushed and his eyes narrowed as he growled. "You're right. We do speak the same language." His hardness was unmistakable against Oscar's thigh. "Whatever work this relationship takes… goddamn, is the sex worth it. And the romance, I guess," he teased.

"As an afterthought?" Oscar smirked at him as he teased.

Roman drew a deep breath and shook his head. "No. I wanted your body before I realized I could have your heart, too. When I first dared to hope… I never got it out of my mind. I don't think I ever will."

It was the most romantic thing he'd heard Roman say. "Kiss me."

Roman laced their fingers together, pressing Oscar's hands into the bed and doing exactly that. His lips were warm and pliant against Oscar's mouth, his tongue darting along sensitive skin before he nipped Oscar's lower lip.

Oscar moaned his approval and hooked his ankle around Roman's thigh, grinding slowly against him.

"Your knee's better." Roman noticed which leg he was using even in a hot and heavy moment, which made Oscar's heart hurt with how protected he felt. "Don't strain it, though."

Oscar smiled fondly at him and pecked his lips. "I'll take care of myself," he promised. "I have to be in teaching shape in January, after all."

"That's right," Roman approved, squeezing Oscar's fingers between his own. "And we have a lot of kinky sex positions to try."

Oscar laughed again. "Priorities." Now that Roman had unwound from the stresses Oscar hadn't even known he was carrying, he was back to his usual self, and Oscar loved every second of it.

"You, romance and sex with you—don't ask me to rank those two—and I'm sure there are other things I forget right now." Roman pretended to furrow his brow in thought.

"I wouldn't dare," Oscar smirked, wiggling his fingers between Roman's until Roman redoubled his grip. "Not when this started with…"

"No strings attached?" Roman laughed. "Goddamn, you snuck a tow rope in there." He shifted his weight to grind against Oscar in slow, rolling motions.

Oscar wasn't sure he'd ever laughed so much in bed. His laughter was only interrupted by a moan when Roman found an angle that let their cocks rub against one another.

Frottage sounded pretty damn good right now. Even dry-humping had found a new lease on life with Roman. He could do it for fucking hours and be happy—if frustrated, but that didn't preclude happiness, either.

Oscar's toes curled with pleasure when Roman let go of his hands at last to start tearing their clothes off. He would have helped, but Roman was clearly delighting in getting them naked as fast as possible.

Then, their hard cocks brushed again, this time with nothing in the way.

Oscar moaned in pleasure, the dampness from Roman's cock sliding over the head of his own cock. Every drop of moisture went a long way when Roman's thick shaft spread it across his with each thrust of his hips.

"Yes," Oscar panted, grabbing the sheets and trying to keep his hips still so Roman could keep sliding the most sensitive parts of their shafts together, the heads rubbing gently but providing firm enough friction that his skin crackled with electric need.

"I want you so bad," Roman whispered, shifting his weight carefully so he could kiss Oscar, his forearm braced by Oscar's head. "So damn bad, all the time."

"Fuck me," Oscar breathed out. "I want you in me. Please."

Roman smiled gently and kissed Oscar a few more times. "Let me finger you first, then."

Oscar gulped, tingles of pleasure fading as Roman shifted off him to grab lube. He swallowed his moan of protest, anticipation making it easier to bear.

He shouldn't have been surprised to find Roman's mouth on his cock for the second time that day as Roman's thick finger slid gently around his sensitive hole and inside. Being filled and enveloped at the same time blew his mind, and words disappeared for a minute.

Oscar tried not to thrust into Roman's fingers as they rubbed his prostate gently, his cock hardening at the teasing. "F-Fuck," he finally managed, impatiently thrusting his hips. "Come *on*. Please."

"I love you. I love how open you are," Roman murmured. "I hope you're never afraid to say what you want again. Ever."

"Whatever it is?" Oscar murmured, his thoughts still hazy.

Roman smiled warmly. "Whatever it is."

"Good. I want that big, sexy dick in me as many times tonight as the first time we fucked."

"Oh!" Roman grinned. "I can't wait to fill that request tonight, as it were."

"Fill it over and over," Oscar smirked. "Any night you want."

"Most nights, now that I'll be here more," Roman nodded, looking smug as hell. "I hope you're ready."

"I'm always ready for… oooh!" The hot, thick tip was sliding inside, and Oscar lost his breath for a moment as he pushed against it.

Finally, Roman was seated inside, pulling Oscar's legs over his shoulders.

Oscar ran a hand over his chest and stomach, conscious that he didn't look quite like he had when they'd first fucked, but Roman pulled his hand away, kissed the palm, and raised it above Oscar's head to press his wrists into the bed again.

"Yes," Oscar hissed as Roman started moving in a slow, steady rhythm in him. "Fuck! Add that to the anytime list."

"You like me pinning you down and fucking you like my beautiful, irresistible, gorgeous, smart, driven, sweet boyfriend?"

Oscar blinked rapidly and cleared his throat. "Trust you to make that romantic."

"I try," Roman winked. He moved his hips in a slow, rolling motion, alternating thrusts and teasing circles of his hips.

Filled and held in place by Roman, his body covered and sheltered, his cock aching for touch but his skin sparking with pleasure nonetheless, Oscar was certain he'd discovered the deepest bliss there was.

When he was ready for more, he didn't even have to ask Roman twice. "More."

Roman grinned. "Whatever you want, baby." His thrusts were harder now, angled just right to hit the pleasurable spot inside that made Oscar squirm with every plunge of Roman's hips against his.

He had no idea how long it had been, but he didn't want it to stop. If it had to, he wanted it again as soon as possible. Just having Roman's firm grip on his wrists, his other hand tight on Oscar's hip, made his head whirl with pleasure.

"I might... not even need a hand," Oscar admitted, his cheeks flushed as he laughed. "I've daydreamed so much."

"Just imagine my mouth on your cock like earlier," Roman whispered into his ear, pressing kisses along his jaw and behind his ear, then his throat. "Me on my knees in front of you, worshipping that gorgeous cock, swallowing it tightly in the back of my throat..."

His cock was swelling, hard as hell and sensitive to the slightest touch as his breath caught in his throat. "Nnh— Roman..." he managed around his grunts and moans. "I'm gonna... oh, fuck. I can't stop. I need to come."

"Do it, baby. You're so beautiful," Roman breathed out. "I'm gonna come any second. I've been thinking about making love to you all evening. Come for me...!" His last words were strained, his expression taut.

Oscar gasped at the beautiful sight of Roman quivering on the edge of orgasm. The image was unforgettable, and the sexuality and intimacy of that moment seared through his nerves. "Yes!"

He rolled his head back as Roman mouthed at his throat, crying out loudly as his own wet, warm passion made a mess between them both. Moments later, Roman's hips shuddered and stuttered as Roman gasped his name, and Oscar forced his eyes open to watch those beautiful expressions of pleasure.

"Oh, fuck," Roman gasped, his grip loosening on Oscar as he guided his legs back to the bed. "More of that, please."

"Just what I was thinking," Oscar chuckled deeply, pulling Roman down against him and wrapping his arms tightly around his back.

Roman kissed him idly as each of them caught their breath. "At least twice more, if memory serves."

"It does serve," Oscar giggled, pressing kisses against Roman's lips playfully now. "And at least one of those times was up against a wall."

"Don't push—" Roman started to say, then cleared his throat. "Sorry. I'll let you be the judge of that."

Oscar beamed and hugged Roman, tangling all their limbs together. "I love that you care."

Their bodies were slick and cooling, but the warmth between them was impossible to walk away from. Oscar had no intention of letting Roman go, messy or not. Tomorrow was for cleaning up—the bedroom, his work life, the new studio, whatever it took.

Tonight was for them and only them.

Epilogue

OSCAR, TWO MONTHS LATER

"Okay, that's all for today. Sorry we ran a little over time there," Oscar apologized, glancing at the clock on the pale lavender wall of the studio. "You were all doing so well I didn't want to stop you before the routine was finished."

He wrapped up the class the same as the rest—congratulating individual students who had progressed in even these three classes, answering questions, and assigning homework to a couple of students who wanted to learn more about moves that had challenged them.

He'd already figured out that adults were a challenge in some ways to teach, having more hang-ups, but the ones who were eager to learn were a joy.

"Matt can help you register for a trial class at the front desk," he promised a student who was asking about taking a second weekly class with him.

"Yo," Matt greeted, waving as he leaned on the door between the bright front reception and the more carefully-controlled environment of the studio. "Follow me up there."

A few minutes later, when the last of the students had packed up and left, Oscar joined Matt at the front desk. "So?"

"Three students. It's a start," Matt told him with a bright smile. "I know it's not a great start compared to you, but... letting us live here for free is more than I could ever ask for."

"It's a start," Oscar shook his head. "My class is just about full anyway. I don't think I can take on more than one more without teaching quality suffering. I'll start sending other students over to you."

"I didn't expect there to be such a demand," Matt admitted. "You saw something here. Anyway, I'm ramping up the Facebook ads, and emailing the newspapers again today."

"See? It's not letting you and Ben crash here for free. You're earning your keep. As soon as you start promoting *your* classes..."

"Yeah." Matt drew a breath, then high-fived him. "Right. Go have lots of kinky Valentine's sex, you animal."

Oscar lit up with a grin. "You too. No more holes in the wall, or you're learning to drywall."

"Yeah, sorry about that," Matt laughed, but he didn't look it.

"Liar," Oscar winked. "See you tomorrow."

His smile was bright as he trotted down the street to his car. He had to get home a little early today so he could start supper in time for it to be ready when Roman was home from work.

It was *his* home now, too. Enough of his personal effects had snuck into their shared spaces, and Roman had eagerly made room for them. The guest room seemed like a long-ago memory.

Supper wasn't quite out of the oven when the door

rattled and Oscar jumped. Roman was early? How inconvenient.

"Hey, honey. I'm home," Roman called out.

He not-very-secretly liked being greeted at the door, so Oscar shrugged off his underwear and tossed it into the laundry bin. Naked behind the apron, he strolled up to the front door to greet Roman. "Hi, lover."

"Oh. Oh, *hello!*" Roman was carrying something behind his back. He glanced up. "Something smells good."

"And it's not just you." Oscar stretched onto tiptoe and kissed Roman thoroughly before letting go. "So? What are you hiding, Mr. Slick?"

"Takeout," Roman admitted and laughed. "Oops." In his other hand, though, he had a bouquet.

Oscar peeked in the bag, then leaned down to sniff the bouquet. He beamed at Roman in approval of his choices and leaned in to kiss him again. "They're gorgeous."

"The food or the flowers?"

"Both. You're home early, though. Did you break the air speed limit? No, don't explain plane speed limits to me," Oscar held up a hand as Roman drew a breath. "Not until after the great sex."

"When you're going to sleep, you mean?" Roman grinned.

"That's right."

Roman laughed. "Whose supper do we eat? We should schedule this next year, who's doing it."

"How about both?"

"Combine… beef and mashed potatoes… with Thai?" Roman grinned. "Sure. Why not?"

"It's *our* Valentine's. It can't be quite normal," Oscar pointed out.

Even after two months of living together, Oscar felt young at heart every time he and Roman laughed together.

Roman found a vase for the flowers and set them up between the candles, and Oscar rearranged the dishes on the table, the pair of them working in sync and anticipating each other's movements easily. Squarely in the center of the table sat the merlion salt and pepper shakers from Singapore.

By then, it was time to pull his supper out of the oven as Roman portioned takeout onto their plates.

"Perfect," Roman declared when Oscar sprinkled salt and pepper across their meals with a flourish. "And I'll get the wine."

Gazing across the table with its unconventional meal to the utterly beautiful man on the other side, Oscar's heart swelled with the deep joy that, once upon a time, he hadn't even dared to hope for himself.

And now the love they'd made was real, and deeper every day, and he would never trade it for anything.

Life was perfect.

SIGNIFICANT BROTHERS #4

"I'VE GIVEN UP ON MY FAIRYTALE ROMANCE."

Forensic investigator Dustin has been single for way too long. His family wants him to find Prince Charming—or at least Mr. Own Job and House—but all he can seem to get are hookups.

Just when he gives up on being swept off his feet by a knight in shining armor… Leo walks in and saves him.

After finishing his tour of duty, Leo is searching for the missing pieces in life's puzzle. The forensic photographer has a heart of gold behind his muscles, but he can't figure out why he doesn't click with women. His first clue comes when he accidentally walks into a gay bar and finds a cute, shy nerd who needs to be rescued.

Things start falling into place, and fast. Leo is a man with a mission to win Dustin's heart. Even as he figures himself out, he won't let anything stop him. Every fairytale has to start somewhere… why not the bedroom?

All they have to do is get over their insecurities and admit to each other—and the world—what they really want.

About the Author

E. Davies writes feel-good, low-angst romance that never fades to black when the going gets good! Born in Canada, after 16 moves and counting, Ed has finally put down roots in north London.

He emerges from his writing nest to coo over fuzzy animals, flee from cute guys, dance through the streets with his chosen family, put together fierce looks, and—most of all—befriend local flowers.

You can find all available titles at: www.edaviesbooks.com

FOLLOW E. DAVIES ONLINE:

amazon.com/author/edavies
bookbub.com/authors/e-davies
facebook.com/edaviesauthor
goodreads.com/edavies
instagram.com/edaviesauthor
x.com/edaviesauthor

Grind

Brooklyn Boys:

Electric Sunshine

Live Wire

Boiling Point

F-Word:

Flaunt

Freak

Faux

Forever

Freedom

After:

Afterburn

Afterglow

Aftermath

Shared Universes:

Shelter

Adore

Miracle

Redemption

Limelight

Barely Regal